The Feline Detective

Clare Hayes

Published in 2012 by FeedARead.com Publishing – Arts Council funded

Copyright © The author as named on the book cover.

First Edition

The author has asserted their moral right under the Copyright, Designs and Patents Act, 1988, to be identified as the author of this work.

All Rights reserved. No part of this publication may be reproduced, copied, stored in a retrieval system, or transmitted, in any form or by any means, without the prior written consent of the copyright holder, nor be otherwise circulated in any form of binding or cover other than that in which it is published and without a similar condition being imposed on the subsequent purchaser.

A CIP catalogue record for this title is available from the British Library.

For my family

Chapter One - George Street	1
Chapter Two - Talltrees	6
Chapter Three - Aristocatcy	12
Chapter Four - The Hunt	17
Chapter Five - Death in the Forest	20
Chapter Six - Interviews	25
Chapter Seven - Polly Marmalade	30
Chapter Eight - The Dragon Inn	34
Chapter Nine - Lucy won't play billiards	38
Chapter Ten - Tangleburr village	44
Chapter Eleven - Thistletongue: master of Law	49
Chapter Twelve - some curious letters	53
Chapter Thirteen - the missing diamond	61
Chapter Fourteen - Mitzy's	67
Chapter Fifteen - The Savoy Theatre	73
Chapter Sixteen - The Hen's egg returned.	79
Chapter Seventeen - Family trees.	83
Chapter Eighteen - Highoak Manor.	87
Chapter Nineteen - Three Blind Mice	92
Chapter Twenty - the Aldwych Dancing Rooms	98
Chapter Twenty One - Danger at the Docks	104
Chapter Twenty Two - Miss Marmalade again.	110
Chapter Twenty three - the Blue Lion club	115
Chapter Twenty Four - the Wedding	121
Chapter Twenty Five - a note from a Lady	126

Chapter Twenty Six - Talltrees again   130
Chapter Twenty Seven - Lucy must decide   135

Chapter One - George Street

Toby and I strolled together through the park, each lost in our own thoughts. My thoughts revolved mainly around the likely nature of the supper Mrs Neatwhisker would have prepared for us, and little about my medical cases. Toby had spoken hardly a word since I arrived, and I feared he was bored again for lack of an interesting case of his own.

As we turned towards Toby's apartments on George Street, Toby was first to speak. "I suspect, old friend, that we have a visitor"

"What makes you say so?" I returned.

"Because her monogrammed coach is waiting - rather too indiscreetly - at the end of the street" answered Toby. And with that he stepped lightly - and with a lifted mood - up the stairs and through the flap.

Mrs Neatwhisker (I have never dared to ask that formidable lady's first name) greeted us at the door. "Oh Mr Hunter, I have put the Lady in the sitting room - she was quite insistent she would see you. I have given her tea but I fear she is quite distressed. Oh, good afternoon Mr Gentlepaw".

"Good afternoon"

"And good afternoon Mrs Neatwhisker. I do hope that our distinguished guest has not finished all of that excellent crumblecake." Although occasionally quite abrupt, Toby had somehow the knack of making Mrs N quite kittish. She scampered down to the scullery as we went through to greet our visitor.

"Milady, we are honoured", said Toby, dipping his tail "But to what do we owe the honour?"

I was stunned - in front of us, sipping neatly on a cup of buttermilk tea, was Milady Celia PinkPaws, debutante of the previous season and sometime talk of the scandal sheets. She was more amazingly beautiful in the fur than any picture could convey. Long lashes framed her enormous ice blue eyes. Her delicate cream fur was

Chapter One - George Street

set off by chocolate pointing, and a short blue silk pelisse graced her shoulders.
"Mr Toby Hunter, and Surgeon Gentlepaw, I assume?"
"The very same. But come, Milady, what brings you to George Street?"
"I am very afraid for someone... someone very precious to me, Mr Hunter. I - oh I hardly know where to begin." Milady Celia sat lightly on the armchair, gently tapping her tail against her hind paw.
" Please do not be distressed. And you may speak quite freely in front of my colleague. He has been trusted with many a secret before now. I believe Mrs Neatwhisker here must surely have finished refreshing our cups, so why not begin at the beginning." For that good lady Mrs N had been fussing about with fresh tea and crumblecake while Celia faltered her words. On this encouragement however she briskly left the room.
"Very well then, at the beginning it was very simple. You see - I fell in love." Truly, if I had believed the scandal sheets of last season, this was not hard to imagine. Milady Celia had caused quite a sensation in the London salons, for she had money and nobility to add to her beauty, and many an ambitious Mama had pressed forward her willing son to promenade with the female scion of the Pinkpaws. Amongst these many willing offers, one young tom would surely catch her eye. And indeed he had - The KitDuke Julius Greatclaw was quite an equal catch in his own way - rather more nobility than money, perhaps, but the papers had made the most of the romance. I imagined both mamas were very happy with the match. If it was truly a love match, too, then that was cream on the milk.
"Of course, in my position, Mr Toby - one - well, one cannot afford to fall in love with quite whoever one pleases."
Hunter gave a slow noncommittal blink. I knew, in fact, of his liberal views on pedigree. He was something of a romantic, but many of

Chapter One - George Street

our cases came from the aristocatcy, and he usually managed to be diplomatic in their presence.

"But Julius and I - we saw nose to nose at once. He is such a wonderful cat. So dignified, and a marvellous sportsman."

I stared firmly at my notebook, scratching a few cursory notes with my foreclaw. Beautiful she might be, but if the lovely Celia kept gushing like this about an idle young kit like Julius Greatclaw, even Toby might not maintain his decorum.

"Greatclaw proposed then?" Hunter was indeed impatient for the nub of the story.

"Oh! Well, yes - we are betrothed. He gave me a family heirloom collar, you see." And Milady loosened the pelisse to expose the gemstars in a silvery collar, just taut around her neck.

"Charming. So what then - he wants to cry off?"

"Oh certainly not!" Milady flicked her tail with some vehemence. " No, Julius is still an absolute gentleman and quite sure of me. But - oh Mr Toby I am so worried that someone is trying to kill him!"

"Ha!" Toby shot me a steely look. " Now we have it. So what occurred - sporting accident?"

"No, it was really very strange." Milady Celia studied a perfect chocolate paw, nervously. "It was at my birthday party. We were having such a wonderful time. Mama had made such beautiful arrangements, the music, amusements and so forth. Even icemilk, which I'm sure Milady Blueclaws won't have at her party..."

Really, I liked Celia less and less as she talked - she even seemed less beautiful as each self-regarding word dropped from her delicate teeth.

"... but when he saw that letter under his plate he looked so pale and frightened - and he wouldn't tell me what was in it."

Toby was crouched forward on the firestool, intent on her words. I only now realised we were at the crux of the matter.

"He was so terribly strange and angry - for days and days. Insisted it was nothing. And Mama too - said that I mustn't fuss about him, just a bit of flu, and perhaps the excitement. And then he has been

Chapter One – George Street

so very mysterious - and these strange letters keep arriving that I'm not allowed to see."

Toby was interested - but not persuaded. "Well, Milady - I am sure your Julius has his matters of business - you cannot expect that he will tell you everything...."

"Oh but this isn't a matter of business, is it?"

And Celia plucked a small letter from her purse, and handed it to Toby. It was charred at the edges, but a few words could still be read at the centre of the page, which had been screwed into a ball. "...won't wait... your ..ife... danger.... or else...."

Toby was by now digging his claws into the very cloth of the firestool, as he stared with deep concentration into the firegrate. Mrs N would scold me later - for she would never scold Toby for such uncouth behaviour. Milady could not see his intense eyes from her perch and was unsure of his interest, so prompted him again.

"Mr Hunter, Mr Toby - you will help me, surely. I simply must marry Julius - but I can't bear for him to be unhappy like this."

"Where did you get this letter?"

"It was the last one to come - yesterday morning with the post to Talltrees before Julius left for town. He set it alight and threw it in the grate, but I lingered in the room after he left. What do you think it means? I cannot make it out."

"It means... trouble. But I cannot help wondering how your fiancee feels about your consulting me?"

"Oh he doesn't know. I thought - well I was sure that he would not like it. But if you can help him - get him out of whatever trouble it is - perhaps it might indeed be a matter of business of some kind? or even gambling? I could bear that. I am sure that he will forgive me." Milady Celia lowered her gaze, demurely showing to powerful effect, as I'm sure she knew, her very long lashes.

"Well I am sure you know young Julius best, Milady. How could he fail to forgive you anything?" Hunter could be brilliantly charming when he wanted to be, and elicited a gentle purr from

4

the lady. He was a very handsome cat himself, with tigerish, tabby markings and a pure white throat and nose. Though well into the prime of life, he had not married, seeming to take far more delight in the solving of mysteries at large, than the greater mystery of the female cat. "When shall we come to Talltrees?"

"You will come then? Marvellous. I must be back tonight but could you come down at the weekend? Mama is throwing a hunting party for myself and my brother, Cecil, you know, so there will be quite a crowd and you could blend in easily."

"You may expect us Saturday morning. We'll take the night-coach."

"We? I am not too fond of a hunt - prefer mending bones to breaking them." I mildly rebuked my friend in this manner - he assumed I would go. But fairly I should have been quite cross if he had not let me come. We generally shared in his adventures, though I added little to the solving of them, but Hunter and I got along well, and we were rarely parted in a good mystery.

"Certainly it is we, Gentlepaw - it sounds like Talltrees is more dangerous at present for cats than mice, and you know that I cannot go into a tight spot without you".

Chapter Two - Talltrees

As Mrs Neatwhisker showed Milady Celia out, Toby bounded straight to his bookcase left of the fire, and pulled out a large red volume. "Pooter's Nobility. I think we had better consult Pooter - my memory cannot retain the complex meanderings of these aristocratic lineages."

"Your memory would be up to it if you liked to retain the information" I grumbled, still pretending to be annoyed at his presumption. But Hunter was ignoring me, intent on the red book.

"Ah yes, I thought so - here we are. The Greatclaws, of course, are legendary. Old Duke Greatwhisker himself, noble already and elevated in rank after the Battle of Hounds' Corner in the Great Dog War. Allied with the Hardclaws by marriage - great beauties, though by rumour somewhat lacking in moral fibre. And their issue becoming the first rank of the Greatclaw family. That great noble London family that has rarely seen the need to amend its surname (finding no more noble addition to it available) ever since. I suspect they shall amend it in their coming merger with the Pinkpaws though - ten generations on the Greatclaw fortune is not what it was, and cannot afford to bare its teeth at the immense fortune of a Pinkpaw seed merchant. Their issue will be Greatpaws, no doubt! If there are any, that is." And Toby snapped the book shut with a flick of his wrist.

"What do you make of her, Robbie?" Few people called me by my personal name, but Toby Hunter was one of them.

"She? Quite the sly little miss, isn't she. Seems as bothered by the quality of the trimmings as the fellow she's marrying. But she does seem genuinely worried about Greatclaw. Why else would she come? Perhaps it is a love match after all?"

"Perhaps" tutted Toby, curling on the firestool, "but also perhaps the scion of the Pinkpaws does not wish to bestow her very lovely

Chapter Two - Talltrees

person and her fortune on a cat - however much he will be a Duke - with an alarming and unknown secret. Even a KitDuchess does not wish to be murdered in her bed."

"Murdered? You do believe his life was attempted then?"

"I believe nothing yet. Something is amiss there, though, no doubt. We must get to Talltrees to discover what it is."

We caught the nightcoach from ParkTower out to the East. I am never completely comfortable in a coach and expected to sleep badly. Coaches on the ParkTower East line were run by an Alsatian family - they spoke little cat but ran a reliable, clean service, and had quite moderate prices.

"Begs? You hef begs?" gruffed the coachdog.

"Just these -we'll take them inside with us" I answered, gesturing at our backpacks.

"Wuff. Ve go now then. Just you tonight." and the Coachdog nosed and shouldered his way into the harness as we clambered aboard. He would need our assistance at the other end, of course, but like many dogs seemed not to find it undignified. It is a double edged sword to have the sensibilities of a cat. We have our refinements, but there are things we cannot bear to do for ourselves.

However the Alsatian's coach was quite marvellously refined. Some ingenious mechanism whereby the body of the coach was suspended from a frame, rather than sitting direct upon the wheels, insulated us from the usual joltings of the road. Hot bricks warmed the seats, and we had the option of a shielded candle to light our journey if we wished. I awoke many hours later to find it past dawn, and our journey nearly over. Toby was awake - whether jolted or not he slept far less when on the scent of an interesting case, and was sat upright staring into space.

"Ah, good morning, Surgeon! Any thoughts on the case?"

"My thoughts are entirely of breakfast," I answered, rummaging in my bag for the lunchbox, "but I see that your mind has been occupied with loftier things. I wonder if I can distract you with some of Mrs Neatwhisker's excellent cured sardines?"
"You cannot distract me, Robbie, but I will certainly eat one!" and saying so Toby batted one from my hand and began to nibble at it while he outlined his thoughts.
"Why should someone want to kill the very noble KitDuke Julius Greatclaw?"
"Money, I suppose?"
"But money is just the thing that the Greatclaws are so sadly running short of. It could still be money, but if so an amount of money that means more to a pauper than to a cat of moderate means. Unless... still it is too early for obscure theories. So probably not money. Jealousy, perhaps? Milady Pinkpaw is a very beautiful young cat, as I saw that you observed very closely."
"I could hardly fail to do so when she was sat a yard away from me. Yes, jealousy seems quite possible. But where to begin to look? She must have had a hundred suitors last season. And from her image in the papers, many more surely admired her though they would not be accepted in suit."
"Quite so, but how many of them were invited to her birthday party? What ho, I think we are here!"
Indeed while we spoke the coach had ceased to move, and the Alsatian was already nosing open the side door. We gathered our things and jumped down.

Talltrees mansion was a very magnificent home. The carriage drive swept around in a half-crescent in front of the house, flanked by the tall beech trees of the mansion's name. The house was symmetrical, with long wings either side of the entrance. The entrance itself was in formal style, with steps up to the front door, and pillars framing high antique double wooden doors with handle ornaments over the discreet flaps. But as we strolled towards the steps, the doors swung back to create a full opening at the front of the house.

We were not the only ones to be arriving. In fact the drive was thronged with carriages. At the front door, Lady Corcinda Pinkpaw herself sat very upright beside her daughter, greeting a line of guests. Her tail bobbed lightly at each answering tail, and for some more honoured guests a dip of her head hinted at a nosegreeting.

Lady Corcinda Pinkpaw looked the very model of aristocratic beauty. Her dark blue eyes flashed between slow blinks at her visitors, as her long laquered lashes swept up and down. The very palest sleek cream fur was set off by just the faintest chocolate pointing on her delicate ears, and by her long nose tipped in delicate pink. She sat upright, sternly still, barely tilting her head as her tail bobbed gently at each arrival. A fine brown silk cloak, lined with fur, and clasped with a gold brooch draped closely over her shoulders and pooled on the floor at her feet. We joined the queue on the steps. Lady Corcinda seemed to be whispering furiously to her daughter about something between greetings. She was a cat of late middle age, past the point of her greatest beauty, but still very handsome. Her dark eyes looked sharply along the queue on the steps from below the thick sweeping lashes.
"Something amiss you think Hunter?"
"I suspect that our delightful visitor has not fully prepared her mama for our arrival. Let us see…" and Toby stepped onto into the hallway to meet the forbidding Lady Corcinda.
"My Lady, it is a pleasure and an honour to meet you," he said, dipping his tail very low, "I am sure your daughter mentioned how very flattered my friend and I were at her kind invitation."
"Indeed, though she has only lately mentioned it."
It seemed that Toby's usual charm would be slower to melt this hard frost.

Chapter Two - Talltrees

"My daughter is very generous and impulsive in nature. She is less clear about the capacity of a simple country home to accommodate guests on a hunting weekend." Lady Corcinda, it seemed, did not mince her words! "However, I am happy to accommodate my daughter's friends for the evening. I regret Mr Hunter, that you and your companion will be obliged to leave us on the return coach tomorrow night. "

"Your ladyship is most kind." answered Hunter, and pushed me into the house while my jaw remained dropped.

"Extraordinary thing!" I gasped. "Member of the aristocatcy, to show so little hospitality to a guest!"

"As she pointedly remarked," said Toby, " Her daughter's guests. Still you are right, I think that Lady Corcinda was more than usually displeased to see us. The nobility tend to show me far more courtesy. Especially when I am returning their jewels, or extricating their progeny from unfortunate liaisons. There is something very curious here. But let us explore."

A black and white butlercat, with a white bow tie, and a natural white throat so pure he was in no need of a bib, showed us up to our rooms. It was merciful indeed that he did, and we had to take careful note of the way, for they were at the very far end of the west wing of the house, and required navigation of two internal stairways. The butlercat, who introduced himself briefly as Mr Furry, said nothing for the duration save to draw our attention to a case of egyptian curios, part of the famous Pinknose collection.

The whole of the house was maintained in classic and expensive style. Our chambers were smallish, but comfortable, with a shared sitting room for our private use. I drew back the curtains on the rear window, overlooking the extensive grounds. In the distance, I could see a pair of grazerrabbits hopping over the lawns, and nearer by large red rose-bushes in neat flower beds.

Chapter Two   Talltrees

Toby joined me at the window. "I see that you are admiring the grounds. But not I think as intently as they are inspecting us." He gestured towards the furthest rose bush and I saw, where I had not noticed it before, the face of a tortoiseshell cat staring up at us, intent with an expression of malevolent rage.

Chapter Three - Aristocatcy

I awoke the next morning in my chamber at Talltrees to find Toby batting at my face. "Come quickly, Robbie, we must be up and about before her ladyship decides to find us an earlier coach!"

My sleep had been disturbed by nightmares of the furious cold face we had seen by the rose bush, and confused impressions of the day before. Despite Lady Corcinda's eagerness to see us go, she was clearly conscious of the strange impression we must have made on her other guests, and had decided to present us as an extra entertainment planned for the first day of the hunting party while all arrived and settled in.

Toby Hunter was of course well known in elite cat society - and largely welcomed in it. He was not however, quite one of the aristocatcy. His fur was tabby, in what many found a strikingly handsome pattern - but not of a classical style. He was a large, rugged cat, sleek and powerful though never running to fat. He had done many a vital good turn to the upper and ruling classes - located precious objects, averted diplomatic catastrophes, some of the more lurid aspects of which were reported in appallingly poor levels of accuracy in the gutter press. Toby did have an aristocatic ancestry at least in part, though he would rarely so much as refer to his family. His monopart name, however, betrayed his more humble, if solidly middle class origins. So Toby was something of a celebrity or Bigcat, to use the clumsy vernacular, and could plausibly be explained away by Lady Corcinda as her star turn before the lunchtime jellies arrived. That first morning we mingled with the gentry, each trying to elicit a few crumbs of new information on our case while being pressed for details of Lady Gertrude's missing collar or the tale of The Hound of the Whiskervilles by starstruck debutantes and greying old ladies.

Chapter Three - Aristocatcy

The Pinkpaws had quite a houseful, around thirty cats in all, not counting ourselves or the servants. As they filed in to lunch in the main hall, Toby and I fell back to compare notes.

"Well they may be nobility but they're a salacious lot," I observed. "That grizzled old puss in the motheaten green cape wouldn't stop bothering me about Duke Tallclaws"

"Oh that old business!" laughed Toby, "well I think you must forgive the lady for being interested in how it turned out, I fancy she and he were once betrothed!"

"Good Bast!" I swore, "That grizzled old mollie...?"

"Never mind it now, what have you found out?"

"Precious little I fear. Quite interesting it is though. I suppose you have read in Pooters' already that Lady Corcinda is the second Lady Pinkpaw. The first died in kitbirth it seems, though very little is known of her. Lord Pinkpaw married the Lady Corcinda while the kit was still weaning, perhaps in part to act as mother to her, though she was also a famous beauty, and noble in her own right. Corcinda had her own litter not long after. Milady Celia is in fact stepdaughter, not daughter to Corcinda. The gossip seems to be that Lady Corcinda is very keen indeed to get Celia married off, though she is quite young still, as she is anxious to bring out her own litter in society, and perhaps to trade on the glamorous new connection of the Greatclaws. Julius has several unwed younger brothers, I believe!"

"Excellent work Robbie, I knew some of it but not all. I have heard much the same with a few additions. Lord Charles Pinkpaw was perhaps not the kindest of men. The ruthlessness that built the Pinkpaw fortune was evident in him. In the years after they first married Corcinda was sometimes seen with a bite or claw mark on her face. She would claim a nursery accident, or having fallen from a fence, and would not discuss it. It seems she has no close confidantes - although amongst this crowd here are her friends, such as they are. Since Charles died last year, there have been no more scratches, and far more has been spent on entertainments such as this one. We had better hush for now and enjoy our luncheon."

Lunch was indeed magnificent. If weekend entertainments like this had been more frequent, the Pinkpaw fortune would be required to keep them up. Delicate bone china bowls adorned the table, so wide and shallow they were almost flat (a subtle compliment to the assumed table manners of the company). Strips of fish, seared on one side were garnished with butter formed in star shapes. Savoury biscuits shaped like boats sailed above the fish in a sauce of blue cream. No morsel of food was so large it could not readily be eaten in a single mouthful. Sugarglass cups with pawhandles held lightly watered milk, warmed to the perfect temperature. The round wooden table was spotless, and two butlercats supervised the topping up of cups and clearing of plates.

I found myself surrounded by young girl cats who proceeded to make a game of making me nervous with embarrassment. Hunter seemed to get on famously with a bookish looking lady cat and Milady Celia on the other side of the table. My companions were Lillia, a stepsister to Celia, and her friend Noemi from school. They were full of foolish talk about their teachers, and especially, when they observed my blushes, about boys, and I was glad to see them run from the table out into the garden as lunch drew to an end.

I did however gain one useful piece on information from these silly pusses - the identify of our mysterious observer in the rose garden.
"That must be Per-cy" declared Lillia. Then, ignoring me again to speak to Noemi "you know, the big ugly gardener I told you about!" and they both dissolved into kittish giggles.
"And why was a gardener deserving of a young cat's notice?"
"Big Paws!" squeaked Noemi, and both ran off from the table.

Chapter Three - Aristocatcy

After dinner sipping drinks were provided by the fire. The young kits had left to play, but some two dozen of us remained to mingle. I pursued the gardening line with one of Lady Pinkpaw's eldest sons - or perhaps stepsons.

"Very fine grounds on the house - I was admiring the rosebeds earlier."

"Oh indeed." Cecil Pinkpaw hardly bothered to disguise his boredom, "Not much of a one for plants myself - sisters seem keener on the garden don't you know."

"Well they seem very fine - very well kept, large blooms. You must have a large staff."

"About the usual I suppose. I say you haven't seen Milady Noemi about have you? She promised me she'd watch me hunt..."

And I retired defeated, having pointed young Cecil in the direction of his equally foolish quarry. Hunter was at my side immediately. "Any more to tell, old fellow?"

"Nothing - except that schoolkits get younger and sillier every year."

"I fear it is we who get older my friend! Well I have little more - excepting that Julius is rumoured to be very short of funds - if the Pinkpaw fortune does not come to his aid in short order, the family home may have to go."

"No great hardship - marry Celia and get the fortune."

"Perhaps - but I still see no motive to threaten Julius - and there is something here I do not like - an odd party don't you think?"

"Odd? Well I don't have a deal to compare it with - it isn't every day I go on a shooting hunt."

"Tch - odd mix of invitees - lot of old pusses, to go with Celia's young crowd, not much inbetween"

"Well Lady Pinkpaw is said to be reclusive isn't she?"

"Yes - but she still has friends - not many of them here. Well, we had better get our guns."

"Not for me thanks - I'll stick to my claws if it comes to it."

Chapter Three - Aristocatcy

"Robbie I think on this occasion I will ask you to overcome your squeamishness. I would rather you were armed."

"Really! Good Bast! Well if you insist, Hunter - though I can't see much to be afraid of."

"I hope you are right, indeed I very much hope so." said Hunter, as we loped after the crowd towards the gun room.

Chapter Four - The Hunt

The Hunt crowd gathered in front of the big bay windows at the back of the house - the hunt would set off from here, heading out into the woods beyond. I had, in deference to Toby's wishes, clawed a short shotgun over my forepaw-arm, and I had secreted a few bandages from my travel kit in a pouch in case they should be needed. I was puzzled at his apprehension, though - the crowd seemed quite jolly, buzzing with excitement, sipping at warm creamtoddy, with some of the grizzled elders chewing on an old fashioned wedge of nipbacco.

The Huntleader, Blackie, blew on a jawwhistle to get our attention and outlined the planned route of the hunt. I scanned the crowd, seeing how many I could now recognise. There was Lady Corcinda, looking almost regal in a short mottled hunting cape, and nodding wisely at some slightly older cats. Beside her were Julius and Celia, she rubbing her face affectionately on his shoulder while he padded the ground impatiently. Cecil and a crowd of other youngish cats, some bearing Greatclaw or Pinkpaw features roamed about at the front, while some others chatted with Hunter beside me. Lillia, Noemi and some kittens played with stuffed mice behind us on the terrace.

We were to go straight through the gardens, over the fence, into the forest, following the path for a few hundred yards or so, then branch off left. Meanwhile Blackie and his crew would curve around the front of the forest to the right to beat out possible prey. Any small animals so disturbed should start towards us. Two tough looking Toms sat silently behind him while he outlined the plan, and with a start I suddenly recognised in one of them the tortoiseshell cat - Percy - that we had seen that morning. His expression now seemed quite blank, but I turned urgently to Toby to warn him.

Chapter Four - The Hunt

However I was too late, Blackie blew three sharp jaw whistle blasts for the off, and the hunting crowd, about a dozen of us, set off at a run behind them toward the fence.

We quickly cleared the gardens and I lost sight of Julius - who went ahead with his cousins - and Lady Corcinda early on. Celia looked quite put out to be left behind with the slower cats like myself. Hunter could keep up more easily, but I just had him in sight entering the forest as I cleared the fence.

Ahead of us the forest loomed moistly dark and primal. Blackie, Percy and the third cat introduced to us - with a nod - as Shifter, streaked around in front of it to the right, as more cats streamed in on the central path. I lost even Celia now, and kept pace only with two of the older cats - Lord Henry Longtail, and the portly KitDuke James Wellington.

"Good fun, this, eh?" Wellington puffed to me as we loped along - "I never get to catch much myself these days, but I can sometimes bag one with this", he said, indicating a dangerous looking antique pistol over his shoulder.

I did not reply, partly because I was quite out of puff. The rounds of a medical cat require little more than a brisk walk in London and I don't run much these days. I reflected not for the first time that Hunter must not sleep much to keep so fit as well as solving mysteries! We reached the marker where Blackie had said we should turn, and went left into the darkness of the wood. I felt the familiar quickening of the senses that comes with the darkness, and sensed my companions, more by scent than sight, spreading out away from me in the darkness.

I slowed to a prowling gait, then to a halt, hearing the others do the same, and turned back with my face towards the path, scenting the air and waiting for prey.

I had not long to wait - ahead of us the Huntleader's crew crashed through the forest, driving mice and birds towards us in some number. A fieldmouse brushed past me, squealing in fright and I felt the bloodlust rise. Scorning the gun, I haunched myself ready

Chapter Four - The Hunt

to pounce on the next small creature to pass. I could hear the squeaking and pattering coming towards me, and was almost ready to jump when the first shot blasted through the darkness, and the scent of burnt powder raced through the air. The primal moment was washed from my mind. I don't like guns - never have. I'm not convinced that cats are meant to use them, and I certainly don't like the injuries they do, of which I have seen too many. I sighed and sat back to wait out the rest of the hunt in peace, as scurrying creatures flew past me giving me curious looks as they ran. While the shots rang out, I couldn't be bothered even to bat at the mice as they passed, and decided to stroll up into the forest to see what the catch was.

Longtail held up his prize proudly, a starling with feathers dripping in blood where he had blasted its wing. "Told you I'd bag one!" he boasted. I see little to be proud of in catching prey with a gun, but saw no sense in annoying more of Lady Cordelia's guests and congratulated him on his 'catch'. The Kitduke made a disturbing sight, cleaning fresh blood from his whiskers, he asserted that a gigantic mouse - perhaps even a rat - had been his. Only his own enormous size made me doubt whether this was a lie - certainly he could have eaten it fast enough! But just as he regaled Longtail with the story of his catch - allegedly without the aid of his gun - a terrible scream rent the forest. The scream of a cat in terrible pain. All three of us raced straight towards the sound - coming from the path. As we arrived a dreadful scene met our eyes. Milady Celia, her face covered in blood, her eyes wide and staring howled loudly. Behind her on the path, two cats lay stretched out, both with gunshot wounds. A single pistol lay between them on the path. Furthest away was a tortoiseshell cat, his face horribly disfigured and partly blown away, and in front of him, leaking blood from a shoulder-wound, was Julius Greatpaw.

Chapter Five - Death in the Forest

We all stopped for a moment, stunned at the scene in front of our eyes. Then I remembered my business, and ran towards Julius. It was obvious at a glance that the tortoiseshell cat could not survive his wounds, but Julius seemed considerably more intact. As I got close I began to see him roll his head and moan softly. He seemed to whisper something to Celia, who interrupted her caterwauling briefly to hear it.

I pushed her gently aside, where Longtail caught her and tried to calm her a little, and probed at Julius' wound. He lost consciousness, and I took a broadleaf from the forest floor and began to bind it tight around his shoulder. The pain as the bandage tightened woke him again, and he stared wide-eyed over my shoulder as if he had seen a ghost. I finished my work and turned around to survey the glade.

Behind me a row of cats silently observed the scene. Closest to the path were those who had arrived first; Celia, Wellington and Longtail. Just beyond them were Cecil and two of his friends. and two other other cats I did not know. Hunter was with them, throwing me a grim but affectionate look. To the North, Lady Corcinda stared sharply at us, blinking slowly as if she could not quite believe her eyes. Lady Petronia Bluefur chattered excitedly beside her - but Corcinda seemed not to listen. To the north and further away another two younger cats just arriving on the scene seemed equally astonished. I started a little to hear a voice behind me.

"Percy is done for, My Lady". It was Blackie, with the menacing Shifter beside him. Shifter crouched down next to the body - he stood up, clutching the gun, and tucking something into his pocket.

Chapter Five - Death in the Forest

Corcinda responded to Blackie in a clear, ringing voice. "You had better take Julius back to the house. And then return for him. I will have Bassetts make arrangements"

"Thank you My Lady" said Blackie. It was as if she had ordered him to move a piece or furniture or turnover a potato bed. He seemed unmoved except to betray perhaps a note of gratitude for the proposed assistance of Bassetts' the undertakers.

"I think the rest of us had better return to the house. " She was astonishing - what a formidable cat. "Can he be moved?"

I did not reply for a moment until I realised she was speaking to me.

"Not immediately I think - some sort of stretcher would be best - he has lost a deal of blood. But I do think we had best get him out of the forest to somewhere he can be nursed. Do any of you have tonic about you?"

Predictably, Longtail had a flask of nipjuice, and I splashed a little on Julius' mouth and nose. He spluttered and blinked at me, clearly confused - but his eyes were clear and pulse seemed quite strong. " Do you think you can move?" I asked, gently.

"I - I'm not sure. Where is Celia?" he whispered.

"Quite safe, I assure you. She is with Lady Corcinda" for indeed Lady Corcinda now had a firm grip on Celia's shoulder, and was enjoining her briskly to compose herself.

"Good. I think I can get up." He winced as he rolled himself over onto his hindlegs, but swayed a little as he sat.

"I shall assist you back to the house," I told him, and took a little of his weight on his left side as he limped back towards the house.

Hunter said nothing, but had joined me as soon as Lady Corcinda had spoken. But he moved as we sloped away - pacing towards the terrible sight that lay behind us. Shifter pushed past him, and Hunter held him up for a moment - I didn't hear their words, but Shifter pulled his paw out of his pocket, to exhibit the contents - two spent shells from the gun he had picked up.

Chapter Five - Death in the Forest

...

I left Julius back at the house, in the care of the noble Ladies Pinkpaw and Bluefur - his fiancee being indisposed. At Corcinda's urgings I had given Celia a light sleeping draught. " She is distressed" said Corcinda - "excessively alarmed for her fiancee". She seemed to me to be more frightened than worried, but either way she would take no harm from some sleep, so I obliged. But I was anxious to get back to Hunter and hear his opinion on the matter.

When I returned, Hunter was stood at the foot of Percy's body, lightly scenting the air.

"Well, Robbie" he said, " it is as I feared. Though I must admit this is not the victim I expected to see."

"Indeed? you think it is murder, then? "

"The cat is dead and somebody shot him. However...I wonder if they meant to do it."

"An accident? That is certainly Lady Corcinda's view. She said that a shot must have gone astray and that Percy was very foolish to have wandered into the shooting line. She made no comment on her prospective son in law!"

Toby blinked slowly in thought. "Look here" - and he pointed at a bullet squashed into a nearby tree. "What do you make of this?"

"Shotgun bullet. From the hunt?"

"Yes - there are splinters around the hole so you can be sure it is recent."

"Could it not be an accident? I heard quite a fusillade before Celia screamed."

"You were not firing then?"

I smiled at my friend. He could not help but make deductions.

"Oh I think I have seen enough blood in this hunt." I returned. "Did you catch anything?"

Chapter Five   Death in the Forest

"I was rather too busy observing the hunters" said Toby. "But unsuccessfully, to my eternal regret - I saw nothing but gunsmoke and frightened mice. Nothing of use, that is, except...aha!"
"What is it?"
"Another bullet hole. Two in-fact. Now what about that?"
"What about it? Perhaps the first shot was a miss."
"Oh but these have been here a little while. And I suspect they hit their target. Yet you may speak truer than you know..."
"What rot, Hunter - why shouldn't there be bullet holes in a wood - cats must always be missing their targets when there's a shoot on. And why should anyone aim at a tree?"
"Why indeed? And I suppose this is your gardener?" he added, nodding at the body.
I inched closer, to examine the blasted head. "It must be - I have seen no other cat with tortoiseshell fur since we arrive, bar one of the parlourmaids, and she was much smaller."
Toby started and almost hissed at me - "you are not sure? You cannot vouch for the markings?"
"I - well I think it is him - but you see what has happened to the face. It's - it's a bloody mess! I mean someone that knew the markings would be certain, but I saw him only twice - once just his face in the garden, and then at the start of the hunt.
"Tch - more complications then. But Blackie seemed to know him."
"Yes - he was sure straight away. He should be coming back soon."
"For the remains - well we will speak to him later. Now where did that shot come from?"
"Shot - thought you said there was more than one"
"That I did, Robbie. Come with me." And Hunter paced away from the body, following the trajectory from the bullet-hole he had first found in the tree, past Percy's feet, back across the path and into the forest. Here he stopped and scented the air again.
"What do you see? What can you scent?"

Chapter Five - Death in the Forest

"Well it's all confused - gunsmoke, blood, and -"
"Yes?"
"Well you can tell there's been a hunt - not much more"
Hunter smiled - "Perhaps not much more, but one or two things I think. What about this?" and he plucked a small object from the ground.
"What is it?"
Toby held out his paw - in it was a tiny gold bead.
"Ah, the question, Robbie, is whose is it. And why is it here? Come - we had better make our enquiries before Lady Corcinda decides she can dispense with your services."

Chapter Six - Interviews

As we approached the house again, a small crowd had gathered on the back terrace, muttering quietly amongst themselves. I saw that Lady Corcinda had had the presence of mind to send a maid to offer refreshments to her guests, and I availed myself of a mug of hot sweet tea as I fended off the enquiries as to my patient's health. Hunter pressed impatiently on through the crowd to the back stairs. We headed up to the room where I had left Julius to rest. As we entered, he looked up quite sharply, though he struggled to raise himself, and gave us a curious look, as if he had expected someone else.

"What do you want?" he snapped, "I am in some pain you know."

"That is rather better than the alternative is it not? I believe Percy will feel no more pain. " Hunter was quite stern.

"He is - dead, then. "

"Oh yes - very dead I should say. How did you come to be near him? "

"My gun had jammed - the Huntleaders usually carry grease and a few tools with them, I wanted him to fix it."

"Well then you have been very fortunate and he most unfortunate."

"I suppose so," Julius murmured. "Terrible accident. Does happen now and then, though it's the first time I've seen anyone killed. "

"Oh I do not think it was an accident, KitDuke I rather think that it was an attempt on your life. And from what I hear not entirely unexpected. "

Julius sat upright, though immediately wincing with the pain. "Someone try to kill me? What nonsense!"

"Do you deny that you have been threatened?"

Chapter Six · Interviews

Julius look relieved. "Ha! Silly girl- I suppose it is Celia who has filled your head with that nonsense. I told her at the time, it just a damn business creditor. Nothing for her to worry about. "

Hunter stared at him hard, but seemed half convinced. "And I suppose you can explain the rest of the letters too?"

"Letters?" Now Greatclaw was more blustering. Even I didn't believe him. "Good lord man, I get a lot of letters - narrow it down a bit, can't you?"

"I have been informed that you have been receiving a series of letters which seem to have troubled you greatly."

"Bills most likely. Celia can't seem to pass a day without needing a new trinket of some kind. Now look here, I shall have a stern word with my fiancee - she should not have troubled you with this nonsense, but it is all nonsense you know. Simple hunting accident. And I'll thank you to leave it well alone."

"And so shall I - I think perhaps it is time that you left, Mister Hunter. I wouldn't want you to miss the next coach." It was Lady Pinkpaws.

"Madam. I have just been telling your guest that he has had a lucky escape."

Lady Corcinda fixed Hunter with a hard stare, and was absolutely silent for a beat. "It was an accident. Hunting is a dangerous sport. Julius must rest now."

She herded us out of the room, closing it behind us. As I looked back into the room I saw Julius looking at her, his mouth hanging open in doubt, and a look of real fear on his face.

Hunter was furious. "Stupid cat - she won't have attempted murder in her house because it wouldn't do for the family name! Bast knows the ancient families fairly dripped with blood - but that was in battle and in history and it won't do in a private country house! We shall have a difficult time getting them to talk. Now quickly, let us see if we can find any witnesses with looser tongues

Chapter Six - Interviews

before she sends Shifter to remove us by force! What about Celia?"

"Now look here, Toby" I remonstrated, "Are you quite sure? The poor kit was quite hysterical you know - I had to give her a sedative. And perhaps it could just have been an accident. Are you sure you want to keep antagonising these people?"

Hunter glared at me. "You seem to forget - one cat is already dead, and I strongly suspect that another is in great danger. He is too much of a fool to confide in me, so I must work around him."

We ran along then to Celia's room - I scratched at the door, and a parlourmaid - the pretty tortoiseshell one I had noticed before, came to meet us. Her eyes were almost red from crying. "There, there, I said - you need not fear for your mistress - she will be quite well. She is just anxious for her fiancee."

But the maid simply looked more forlorn, and gestured us in. The room was still something of a kitten's room - a few much loved old toys peered out from the top of the wardrobe. But there were signs too of the noble young lady we had met. Ribbons in many colours curled out of an open box on the dressing table. There were no books, but fashionable magazines were piled in one corner. Daisy sprigged curtains hung at the window, and a thick colourful quilt covered the bed.

Celia was curled on the couch, her pupils still wide and dazed from the sedative. She spoke in a dreamy, mazy voice as if from very far away. She stretched and yawned as we came in.

"Oh hello doctor - I feel ever so peculiar. Have I been dreaming? Is Julius alright now? There was so much blood everywhere..."
She trailed off into silence.

Hunter placed a paw on her forepaw-arm. "Celia, listen to me, it is vitally important that you tell us what you know. Julius may be in great danger. What did you seen in the forest?"

Celia's eyes swam into focus and fixed on Hunter. "The forest. Yes - well you saw that I fell behind from the first in the hunt. I

was annoyed about that. I wanted to hunt with Julius. So I tried to catch up."
"And did you?"
"No - I only caught up to Cecil and some of his friends."
"Who?"
"Um - Peter Wellington, James Pinknose and Harry Greatclaw - that's Julius' brother."
"And you stayed with them?"
"They didn't all stay together. Harry and James went on ahead - they're a bit faster. But Peter and Cecil stayed with me and we had some good shooting. I got a starling. And then I heard shouting."
"An argument?"
"I couldn't make it out - but I recognised Julius' voice. So I ran towards the noise, into the clearing."
Hunter was deadly still - intent on the story. "This is essential, Celia - what did you seen when you entered the clearing."
"That horrid gardener, Percy, he was snarling at Julius - he looked quite frightening. And he was holding a gun. Julius had his back to me but I could tell it was him - and I called out to him and he spun round just as I heard the shots and it - oh Bast it was horrible!"
"Shots? How many shots did you hear? "
"Two or three I think"
"Well which was it? Two or three?"
"I don't know! You don't understand! There were shots all the time from the hunt - but these seemed louder - closer. Two, I think."
"And where did they come from?"
"Well a gun, silly!" Celia hiccuped.
I picked up the medicine bottle I had left. "My dear, you didn't take any more of this after I left, did you?"
"Oh just a little bit of it, doctor, it was making me feel a lot better and I was starting to feel quite anxious again. Polly thought it would be alright." I pocketed the bottle and whispered to Hunter,

as Celia's eyelids started to flutter closed. "Quickly, cat - she'll be asleep in another minute"

"Celia - did the shots come from where Julius was stood or from behind you?"

She yawned. "Oh - one of each I think. I feel ever so tired. Just going to have a little sleep." And with that she curled up and closed her eyes and began to snore.

Hunter paced up and down. "One of each! It can't be! Perhaps when it fell? There's something I don't understand here..."

"Excuse me sirs - but I think that your coach is here" Polly the maid was stood by the door.

"Thank you Polly" I said, sternly, waving the confiscated bottle at her "But may I advise you to be a little more cautious with your mistresses' medicines in future? This isn't cough mixture, you know."

"Oh I'm sorry sir, she insisted, you know." She cast her sleeping mistress a look of mingled affection and exasperation. "Spoilt, you see - she don't get refused much." She blinked away a tear.

"Now come on - no need for that. Oh - I suppose you are upset about Percy. Did you know him well?"

Polly's lip trembled and she let loose a low, sobbing wail. "He was my brother, sir - a bad cat he was, but he was my brother, and now he is gone." And she ran out of the room. Astonished, we followed.

Chapter Seven - Polly Marmalade

There was no sign of Polly as we left the room, but a butlercat approached us carrying our bags. He coughed in an embarrassed manner. "I have taken the - ah - liberty - of packing your effects for you, gentlemen. My lady was anxious that you should not miss the coach."

Hunter looked amused. "How very thoughtful of our hostess. But our reservations are for the night coach - tomorrow night. Perhaps we can divert ourselves in the village for a while?"

The Butlercat looked relieved. He was clearly under instructions to ensure that we left but these did not seem to stretch to ensuring that we returned to London. "Indeed, sir - there is excellent accommodation available at the Dragon Inn in Tangleburr Village if there has been some - misunderstanding. "

"That sounds ideal, er .."

"It's Macintosh, sir"

"That sounds ideal, Macintosh. Can you give us directions?"

"Delighted, sir, I shall show you myself." and Macintosh sketched out the route for us as we headed down to the front steps.

As we got there, a coach swept out of the drive, the anxious faces of Noemi and Lillia peering out at us from the windows. Lady Corcinda was waving them off. She barely looked at us but swept back into the house.

I looked up at the windows as we walked down the drive. Mostly they were blank, save from a top room, where the noble profile of Julius Greatclaw could be seen to observe our departure, apparently unmoved.

"Great Bast, Hunter - what do you make of it all?" I began as we rounded the gate, but he hissed at me to be quiet. A moment later I saw why as Polly darted out from behind a bush in the lane.

"I had to speak to you, sir!" She looked very frightened, but determined too.

Chapter Seven - Polly Marmalade

"I thought as much - how long can you stay away?"

"I'm not sure - it is my afternoon off but as the hunting has been cut short I think we are all wanted back at the house. I won't be missed for a little while yet. "

"Come then - walk with us to the village. You know it? "It is my home, sir. And it was poor Percy's home til he fell out with Papa."

"I see - well you must tell us all about it, Polly. But do call me Hunter."

"That's a funny name."

"It is my second name - but it's what I am often known by. And what is your full name?"

"I am Polly Marmalade, sir, I mean, Hunter, sir"

Hunter smiled at her - "From a long line of Marmalades I am sure."

"Oh yes, sir" Her eyes smiled back "It's not a noble name I know, but we are proud of it."

"And who is we?" You have a big family?

"Oh no, sir, there's four of us now. Ah no, three of us. With Percy gone, bless him. Oh what shall I tell Lucy?"

"And Lucy is?"

"My big sister - she looked after us all really, ever since Mama died. It was just us young ones, Percy and Papa after that for a while. And then Papa was lost this winter. "

"My condolences. He must have been a great loss to you all."

"Thank you - you are kind, Mr Hunter. But to tell the truth he had been ill such a long time. It was sad but it was a relief that he had no more to suffer. We did lose his pension though. Lucy spoke to Percy about doing more to help keep me and my brother William. We are hoping he will go to the city, you see, so we want to try and keep him in school. Percy was a grouch about it but he got me the job up at the house, and then he started to send a bit of money home for us. He won't no more - oh whatever shall we do?"

Chapter Seven - Polly Marmalade

"It sounds like the formidable Lucy will have a plan. Can I meet her?"

"I was hoping to see her myself - I must tell her about Percy, you see. She will be in her work, though, until the evening."

"Yes, I see that. What does she do?"

Polly spoke with glowing pride, "She works in an office - she uses the write machines to make letters for a businessman there. "

"A secretary?"

" I think that's it sir - she don't seem so proud of it but it seems very clever to me."

"I am sure you are right to be proud of your sister. But we are nearly at the village and you have not, I think, yet told me what you meant to."

"Oh sir - well it's Percy you see. I - I heard you talking to his Lordship. You don't think it's an accident?"

"I do not, Polly. Do you? "

"Well I don't understand it Mr Hunter, sir. Percy was a bad cat. He often had scratches from kits he had - upset. And he got in a bad fight once over some gambling debts. He never seemed to keep anything from his wages. But you said that it was Julius they tried to hurt? Percy always seemed so bitter about things, ever since he fell out with Papa."

"I think, so, my dear. I believe that Percy was just unfortunate to be in the way."

"Well then you must catch the cat that did this sir - I know they don't want you interfering up at Talltrees. That lot won't want the noise of it, not with the wedding coming up. They want pink roses and gemstars, not blood and money to be the talk of the day. But he was my brother, sir - and he was a bad cat, but he didn't deserve to die. You must find who did it and lock them up."

Polly stopped us all in our path as she spoke, another tear rolling down her cheek. Hunter looked solemn. "You are quite right, Polly, a cat has died, and another cat took his life. I will not tolerate this thing and I will find the truth of it."

Chapter Seven Polly Marmalade

"Oh thank you sir - that is a relief to me. It will be bad enough but we must know the reason of it. Here, we are at Tangleburr." Indeed, we rounded the last curve of the path to see the cottages of Tangleburr village crowding before us. "The Dragon is just down on the left there." said Polly, gesturing to a side lane. " I must go and find Lucy - shall I send her to you later?"
"Certainly. I shall be delighted to meet her." said Hunter. Polly ran off into the village, and we turned down the lane to find the Dragon Inn.

Chapter Eight - The Dragon Inn

The Dragon Inn was a very ancient building - converted, it seemed, in the very earliest of cat times from Yooman use, the entrances were so lowered as to be almost uncomfortable to slink under. The painted sign outside was very pale and blistered with age -no doubt overpainted many times it did indeed show a green and scaly dragon, defeated by a crushing blow from a tiger. A single great wooden knotted beam formed a dark lintel over the door, and my eyes widened quickly to take in the gloom inside. Rushes, thyme and lavender covered the floor, scenting it sweetly, and a faint breeze blew through the portholes punched in the boarded windows. Round tree-trunk tables and willow benches were tightly packed through the single room, and a low buzz of comfortable chatter was punctuated by the clinking of china tankards.

An elderly and plump tabby approached us as we entered - bobbing her tail, she gestured to our bags. "Rooms, sirs? Will you be staying long?"

"Not long I think - we must be back to London tomorrow evening." said Hunter

"Just the night then - and breakfast? I have lovely smoked kippers and jam. Or there's - eggs?" The mention of London had clearly alarmed our hostess. I interrupted her before her culinary inventiveness outstripped her larder.

"Kippers sounds ideal, madam. Could you show us the room?" Relief flooded her eyes.

"This way, gentlecats."

The old spiral staircase was at the back of the room, just beside the bar, and half-steps inserted for the shorter legs of the ancients almost tripped us as we mounted. Ebbeline, our hostess chattered nervously as we went - but instructively as it turned out.

Chapter Eight The Dragon Inn

"Ah yes, I thought that might have been it," she said "Often when there's too big a party at the hall some of the young gentlefolks' friends will stay a night or two here. They come and play the table billiards too of a night. And some of them likes a jug of beer too! But if I get any trouble I can allus sort them out with a Word. They wouldn't want that telling to their Mamas! Ho no!"

Hunter curled his lip a little but could not resist the chance of more information. "Did you ever have Percy Marmalade stay here?"

"Percy? Dear me no, sir, whatever would he stay here for when he had his own home to go to in the village, and then a nice comfy billet at the Hall in the week, too. He comes here often enough, though. Reg'lar as clockwork when he's a wage to spend. Bad cat, that, if you don't mind my saying, sir. However did a gentlecat like yourself come to know him?"

"I am sorry to tell you madam that Percy died today"

Our hostess, who was just in the act of swinging open the door of our room, stopped and shrieked loudly.

"Oh Dear Bast in Hevven! And me talking of him so unkindly! Well bless him now! Aaah - oh poor Lucy she'll cry for him, though he don't deserve it. I allus knew he'd come to no good! But whatever happened sir? Was it ..." (and I swear I saw her lick her lips) "... was it a Scandal?"

"Shooting accident. " Hunter, who had a strange sense of humour, seemed determined to provoke Ebbeline - perhaps to see just how high a note she could scream. "I regret to inform you madam, that the Noble KitDuke Julius Hunter was also injured in the incident." But this additional information was simply too much for one accustomed to normal village levels of excitement to take in. Ebbeline was dumbstruck, and simply flapped her jaw and waggled her whiskers for a moment quite without an intelligible sound. "The Noble...injured... oh .. well I ...oh! And Percy! Quite dead! Ooooooh! " She sat down right in the doorway and pulled a small bottle of scented oil from an apron pocket, then proceeded to sniff on it deeply. "Well! Well! That's your room then. Well - oh I must go tell... " But Ebbeline was overwhelmed by the very possibilities of who she could tell this quite shocking news. She staggered off down the stairs leaving us to find our own beds. Hunter chuckled to himself as I stared at him as gravely as I could manage.

"Well then, if you've quite finished amusing yourself, " I strictured, " what pray tell are we doing here?"

"Investigating, old boy. I think you heard I had a commission, did you not? "

" I did. Though I don't think you've a client yet that will pay you for the job. "

"Perhaps. I rather think that Celia would be good for the money if she could spring it from her Mama - though I'd scorn to take her pocket money. "

"So long as you do not imagine you will be billing Polly for our lodgings."

Hunter looked grave - "That I do not. She was quite distressed to lose her unworthy brother, was she not? Though even she had to admit he was hardly worth the tears. But I have my cause, Robbie, or rather reinforcement of it. We have a murderer to catch - and one who I think has so far failed to hit his intended prey."

"You are sure then that the target was Julius?"

"The coincidence of his fiancee alerting us to apparent danger - the letters and such - followed straight on by this attack in which he was definitely hurt - seem too much to swallow, don't they? I was shaken by his laughing off of the threats - perhaps Celia's imagination ran a little riot there. I'll tell you for certain he's afraid of something, though I can't say what as yet."

"And who do you suspect? Is there danger even now? Might he not be attacked at the Hall?"

"I think he must be safe tonight. It seems that his murderer wishes him to have an accident of sorts - another too soon would be implausible; unless..."

Chapter Eight - The Dragon Inn

He tailed off, pacing the room and swishing his tail.
"What, Hunter? Unless what? You're making me nervous!"
"I mean unless there was some reason for speed? There must be some reason why the attack was this weekend. Something perhaps to do with the engagement? That reminds me of something that's been nagging at me all day - have you seen the Journal register? "
"I scanned the Journal at breakfast yesterday, but I don't often read the register - too many deaths of old friends and soppy birth and marriage notices..oh!"
"Exactly so." Hunter nodded "I usually make a habit of checking as the information so often proves useful in a case. I suspect there may be something to the purpose there to learn. Well we shall have to check the back issues in the club on our return. Hungry?"
I was instantly ravenous and realised it was many hours since we had eaten. "I should say! That lunch was very pretty on the plate but not much solidity to it, was there? I bet they do a decent dinner here. "
"I expect so", chuckled Hunter, "But I think you may have to wait a bit for dinner - Ebbeline has a whole village to convey news to before she can get to her kitchen." But he saw my dismay - "Perhaps there will be some morsels we can make shift with behind the bar until she returns."
We unpacked our bags and washed our faces. The rooms were small but very cosy, and shining clean. Fresh soft white cotton cushions sat in the couch-beds, and a big jug of cool water and a small cup full of meadow flowers sat proudly on a rough wooden bench under the window. My stomach rumbled however and we tripped back downstairs to beg for roasted sprats from the barmaid.

Chapter Nine - Lucy won't play billiards

We got a corner seat by a punch-window, and a great pile of roasted sprats to nibble with our nipbeer while we waited for Ebbeline to work magic in the kitchen. I shall tell you now that we waited in vain. Kippers there were, but nothing else of note. Ebbeline had clearly long since decided that her talents as an innkeeper did not stretch to gourmet cookery, and her menu was mainly composed of fish both caught and cooked elsewhere.
The early evening atmosphere in the bar was subtly changed. The sun was dropping outside, and a rowdier crowd had begun to gather. Some local mewling kits milled around the billiard-table, batting idly at the balls and practising their trick shots. They laughed at each other when they missed, and hissed in pretended awe at good shots. You may perhaps never have played real old fashioned table billiards with a proper wooden bat. Unlike the sleek baize setups that you will find in town, the traditional bar billiards table, though still round, is plainly made of shaped wood with quite a short lip around the edge to keep the balls inside. The four holes (in contrast to the seven of the town game) are evenly spaced - and traditionally aligned to the four points of the compass. No wooden keeper is used to mass the balls at the centre for the start of the game - they are simply mashed together in a rough mound, and the cue ball dropped in the centre to start the game. If a spotted ball goes first in a hole that side may play on until they miss. There are no leather gloves to hold the round paw-bats in place - a simple leather band is pulled tight through a buckle over the paw, and you must beware for splinters!
I observed the locals batting about for a while, munching between times on some indifferent kippers. There was no use trying to speak to Hunter until he was ready - I could see he was lost in plots and suppositions and would speak when he needed an audience. Ebbeline was speaking in low urgent whispers to a grey,

Chapter Nine - Lucy won't play billiards

miserable and surprisingly thin old cat behind the bar. He had just the gloomy look and nodded enough that I guessed he must be her husband. He went to serve some of the tables nearer the door and I noticed for the first time some cats that I recognised. Cecil and his friends from the hunt. They were chuckling together over mugs of nipbeer and from their wild gestures and hisses I guessed they were comparing exploits from the hunt. I muttered to myself trying to remember the names that Celia had told us. One had the serious looks and chocolate colouring - though a weaker jaw - of Julius - that must then be Harry Greatclaw. Who were the other two then? Didn't she say there was a Wellington? and a - somethingnose?

"Peter Wellington, James Pinknose and Harry Greatclaw" Hunter tapped on my forearm. "Though you could do your staring a little less obviously, old boy - they are like to notice. "

"Could any of them have had anything to do with it? Surely not, Celia was with them when she heard the shot."

"Not quite I think you'll find - in fact if I recall her story correctly any one of them could have taken the fatal shot - though James and Harry are more likely."

"What? Harry try to kill his own brother? And what has James Pinknose to do with it?"

"Well I don't know that either of them did as yet, but there could have been a motive strong enough."

"Such as?"

"Oh, money is the obvious thing. Though if what we've heard is true there's none of that. Or jealousy. If Julius dies before his father then Harry would become the KitDuke - and the centre for attention of every ambitious young heiress. Harry is of that crazed age that every young male cat likes to forget. It could be he admires his brother's fiancee more than he ought. Or…"

But I was not to hear Toby's final theory that night for suddenly he gripped my arm much harder and hissed to me to look to the other side of the door. I could not make it out at first for it was the

Chapter Nine - Lucy won't play billiards

darkest corner with no window at all, but there was some sort of commotion in progress. Two cats were arguing in a way they could not keep quite quiet enough, and one it seemed had just leapt to his feet, kicking away the wicker stool. He hissed loud enough to hear across from the bar,

"Begone then - I don't care if there's a job for me or not no more. I'll have other ways to make a living soon enough, and money to spare."

The cat he was hissing at clicked at him disapprovingly, but evidently decided this was too public a place for any sort of fight. He retorted, deliberately also loud enough to hear, "I'll see you bright and sharp at eight at the manor, or there will indeed be no job for you." and Blackie the Huntleader strode quickly out of the inn, his tail trembling with anger.

"But who was he..." I began.

"Pssht. Be quiet. We aren't here, remember." hushed Toby. I had no need to ask though for a moment later the other cat also stalked out, smoothing his whiskers in embarrassment, and I could see Shifter's great ugly bulk racing away down the path after his employer.

"Going to make amends no doubt - perhaps it was an idle boast. But I bet he's a good shot after all those years of hunting." muttered Hunter.

"Which one?"

"Oh Blackie's the shot, no doubt. I shouldn't threaten to blackmail him! Hunting accidents are it seems none too difficult to arrange."

"You don't think that Blackie...?"

"No, not particularly - but it's interesting that Shifter might think so, if that was what he hinted at. I suppose those two have both seen enough gunshot wounds to know that Percy and Julius were not the simple victims of a jammed shotgun. "

"Ha - well I can make no sense of it"

Chapter Nine - Lucy won't play billiards

"Nor I as yet, there is some fact not yet in place I think. Why kill Julius now?" and Hunter pushed aside our kippers impatiently as he ennumerated the possibilities. "Money - an inheritance? To prevent the wedding? Well, perhaps if it had been already announced and not just an engagement. Jealousy? Revenge?"

"Revenge for what?" I eyed the kippers hungrily and pulled another off the plate as Hunter banged down his mug crossly. "Well what indeed - the trouble is that aside from what we - and the rest of London - read in the Tattle columns, we really know nothing at all about young Julius." He scratched a row of lines in the table with his thumbclaw to emphasise his points. "We don't really know much about his parents - who he has disappointed with this match - or I suspect most importantly, his money. I think we must make some closer investigations when we get back to London."

I nodded, incapable of answering as my mouth was entirely full of kipper. But a moment later I gulped it right down as one of the most stunning creatures I have ever seen appeared in the doorway. Her tortoiseshell colouring was oddly light in colour, more golden brown than orange, and the setting sun behind her shone a halo through and around her fur. Her huge blue eyes blinked and widened in the gloom before she strode purposely straight towards our table.

"You must be Toby Hunter." It is one of my very few regrets in my friendship with Toby that whenever we meet a particularly attractive female I generally get noticed some half hour to an hour after he does. Regrettably I cannot account this only to his fame, for Toby is a handsome cat and can deploy some considerable charm when he wishes to do so.

"That I am Miss - but you have the advantage of me."

"I am Miss Lucy Marmalade. And I believe you have met today my sister Polly."

Lucy had a firm, clear, voice. She seemed rather better spoken, as well as more attractive than her younger sister.

Chapter Nine - Lucy won't play billiards

"So we have, indeed. May I offer you my condolences on the loss of your brother."

"Thank you, sir. Oh, and this must be your friend Surgeon Gentlepaw?"

I mewed unintelligibly.

"Pleased to make your acquaintance, sir. But I fear it must be a brief acquaintance."

I made slightly more unhappy but still incoherent noises. Hunter spoke for us, "I am sorry to hear it Miss, why must it be so?"

"I must ask you not to involve my family in your investigation. Polly confessed to me she had asked you to - in her foolishly dramatic language - to avenge our brother's death. "

"She did - ask something like that. " admitted Hunter

"Well it's quite absurd. Percy was killed in a simple accident. I have spoken to Lady Pinknose myself and she explained it all. Her family have been very good to mine - Polly and Percy are not the first and I hope not the last to be in service there. I do not wish to add to their annoyance with some wild goose chase."

I was shocked out of my stuttering admiration, "Dear me, girl, harsh words don't you think when your brother's dead."

Lucy gave me a penetrating stare. Her eyes were wet with emotion but firm of purpose, "I was not - overly fond of my brother, Mr Gentlepaw. He caused my already troubled family far too much more unnecessary trouble. I am sorry he is dead, but I assure you that worse things than this have happened in my life."

I was quite astonished. And dismayed. This adorable kit seemed to have the stone heart of a lion.

Hunter however seemed almost to smile. "Miss Lucy you need not concern yourself. I see that you are anxious to avoid further uncomfortable interviews at the Great Hall. We quite understand. Your brother's name need not come into it."

Lucy held his gaze for a moment until she was quite convinced he was in earnest. Then turned and without another word walked straight back out towards the door.

Chapter Nine - Lucy won't play billiards

"What a hard nosed little kit!" I exclaimed

"I suspect, Robbie, that her nose had been hardened for her over quite some time. Did you notice the fraying on that bonnet? They have been a very poor family, I think. "

"Well, perhaps so, but..."

And there was the final commotion of the evening. Cecil attempted to stop Miss Marmalade as she made her way to the door. He seemed to be waving a billiards bat at her, and swaying a little tipsily. I half started up from my chair to accost him, but Hunter pressed me down. " I think that Miss Lucy Marmalade will have no need of your assistance. " he said, smiling thinly. And indeed Lucy paused only to swipe the unfortunate Cecil out of her way with a well-judged bat to the nose, before proceeding out into the dusk.

Chapter Ten - Tangleburr village

There was little more excitement in the Dragon Inn that evening. Cecil, perhaps embarrassed by his cut to the nose, drank far too much nipbeer (a very tasty local brew called Tanglepaw) and had to be dragged home by his friends, whilst noisily protesting he was fully alert. Hunter and I laid low, and made an early night of it after our kippers. I must have bumped my head on a low ceiling at some stage for I awoke to the sunrise with an almighty headache, and a very dry throat. I could hear Hunter pacing about already so gave my face a quick wash and knocked at his door.

"Ah come in Robbie - regretting the Tanglepaw? I have given it a deal of thought and I think we might benefit from a stroll in the village before the night-coach comes to pick us up." Hunter can read my face like a book.

"Nothing to do with Tanglepaw. I'm perfectly alright. What can we investigate here though?" I protested.

"Well I gather from our landlady that Cecil and his friends are quite often making a nuisance of themselves in the village. Perhaps we might hear a bit more about Harry Greatclaw. We can't return before this evening in any case."

"True enough. I hear they have quite decent fishing hereabouts?" Hunter brushed my ignobly peckish thoughts away. "I believe there is some sort of brook. But I can't see what relevance that could have.... oh you want breakfast I suppose. Come along then."

Madam Ebbeline provided item three on her extensive menu for our breakfast (eggs - admittedly nice large hen eggs, just slightly overcooked), and we then stalked purposefully into the village. It was about a mile or so in length, mainly ancient converted cottages and shops along the lines of the Dragon Inn, though here and there with a more modern adaptation or remodelling and a very few newer built houses. There was just one cross-street, and no church, though I noticed another two inns. One was a coaching

Chapter Ten - Tangleburr village

inn called the Turbot Arms (I told you there were fish) and another named the King's Head - though which King it had been was impossible to tell from the rotting sign.

We spotted quite easily Lucy's place of employment - the only likely candidate was the solicitor's office - but decided against disturbing her labours. Aside from this office, there was Bassetts (the promised undertakers), an uninventively named 'Turbots' (a fishmonger), a general store selling string, wax, pots and pans and soforth, a grocers and a small outfitters ('Shinytogs') for hats and ribbons.

We found a small tea-shop and settled into a corner in good earshot of any available local gossip. We had not long to wait. Percy's demise was by now quite the talk of the village. And it seemed that Cecil and his friends were quite frequently making a nuisance of themselves in each of the village inns in turn. I shall report the conversation of good Madam Turbot (I doubt this was her real name but it will stand in good stead) and Madam Bassett (I'm pretty sure of this as she was clearly the undertaker's wife) much as we heard it. Although so as not to bore us both I shall omit those parts not strictly relevant to the case.

Turbot: "Well Bess and I suppose your George will be doing the burying of him? Has the big house paid for it or will Lucy be on the borrow again?"

Bess Bassett: "George and I won't loan her for a second funeral not while she h'ain't paid off on the fust one! No, the Big House has paid up handsome. Not that there's a great expense to it. Nothing fancy in the burying - no box or anything. But there was a mess to him and they wanted it very fast done. "

Turbot: "They? Lucy wanted it fast, you mean?"

Bassett: "Oh no, My Lady did. She - well I won't tell you she spoke to Bassett herself - course not. But she sent word by Blackie 'twas to be done all nice and all quickly too. Lucy didn't have no say in the how of it. Why should she when we all know she can't

Chapter Ten - Tangleburr village

pay. Though they'll have less struggle now there's one less mouth to feed."

Turbot: "I thought he mainly drank?"

Bassett: "Oh it's his bookmaker's mouth I'm thinking of!"

---much laughter----

Bassett: " It was the embarrassment I suppose - they didn't want no corpse rotting in shed while they had a houseful of guests. Least said soonest mended I suppose."

Turbot: (showing that she too had connections with the gentry) "Oh indeed I knew there was a lot of them to be there this weekend. They ordered three great salmon to be sent on Friday morning. And two barrels of salted prawns! " This was very irritating - I am very partial to salted prawns. "Did you hear who else was there? I heard that Julius was hurt too in the accident! A worry for his affiancee, that?"

Bassett: (showing her superior knowledge of the strange ways of the gentry) "The KitDuke Julius Greatclaw, you mean? 'Tis true he was injured. Though just a small graze said Blackie. His brother didn't seem too troubled on it - he and young Cecil and that crowd were making riots in the Dragon again last night. Had to be thrown out of it I heard."

Turbot: "It won't have been Norman doing any throwing then. Ebbeline's the one to grab them by their scruffs if they get disordered!"

---more laughter and a succession of observations about the quality and nature of Ebbeline's fur, cookery and husband---

Turbot: "Ah but I don't wonder at Harry not caring too much for his brother. Often I've seen those two dribbling over the same village miss. He's not so much younger, you know. And Julius will get everything when his father dies. There's no love lost there - He'll make his brother work then if his father won't yet."

Bassett: "Pah! There's nothing worth having. That's what Cecil says anyway. He's none too impressed with his sister's doings there. They've promised a great dowry to the Greatclaws to fix her

Chapter Ten Tangleburr village

up with a title. But that's all there is. Terrible debts the Greatclaws have. 'Twas his grandfather began it all - gambling on hound races! No harm when there was a great fortune to play with, but now they're down to selling off their titles to the highest bidder - better that than their silverware and portraits it seems."

Turbot: "I cannot credit that - the Greatclaws stony broke? And why couldn't they sell a portrait or two? Or a bit of land if they were short of money?"

Bassett: "Mortgaged. And the rentals just paying it so they don't have to sell."

Turbot: "Tch. I don't believe you Bessie Bassett. Cecil never told that lot to you. You don't never hear nobility talking like that no matter how much nipbeer they have drunk."

Bassett: (indignant) "I'm telling you, Magda, I've heard it my - well, at least my girl Sibyl heard it - she's behind the bar at the King's Head and picked it up in bits and pieces when Cecil was in there with James Pinknose one night. Quite gloomy he was - family honour or some such. Worried about his own inheritance more like."

Turbot: "Oh, Sibyl - are you sure she wasn't too much distracted by the handsome James?"

Bassett: (now squeakily indignant) "My Sibyl is pleasant, and no more than pleasant to all of the customers, and she's too much sense in her head to have it turned by a silly small-jawed blueblood like James Pinknose. And I'll thank you not to forget it."

Turbot: "There, there Bessie I didn't mean anything by it - that James fancies himself alright, and it's not just your Sibyl he's sniffed around. Even my dear Daisy, though she's had her first litter not two summers past, had to be very sharp with him when he just came in for a necktie!"

Bassett: "Oh and how are your Daisy's kittens coming on? Growing up fast I suppose..."

Chapter Ten - Tangleburr village

--Here the conversation became quite insupportably dull for what felt like an hour before Magda and Bessie exited, well fortified by their gossip and a gallon of tea.

Hunter was thoughtful - nursing a cup of now cold tea, "Well what have we learned, Robbie? Quite a few possible motives there, I think?"

"Were there?" I scratched my chin, sleepily. " Not sure that I see it. If Harry bumped off Julius he'd inherit the title I suppose - but you'd said that before. And I still can't see him attacking his own brother to inherit nothing very much."

"That wasn't quite the motive I meant, old boy. Though that stuff about debts was interesting - we must determine the truth of it for certain. I'm not sure I trust Bessie's Sibyl to be completely reliable in this matter, never mind her mother's good opinion of her. What about Cecil?"

"Cecil? What's he got to do with it? You mean what they were saying about him not wanting Julius for a brother in law? But he'd hardly kill Julius to protect - what? a tiny fraction of his family inheritance?"

"Perhaps not - but I wonder just what deal has been struck between the Greatclaw and Pinkpaw clans. The Pinkpaws have long had a violent streak you know."

"Well I hazard the streak has skipped a generation in Cecil. Or did you not, oh great detective, observe a certain Miss Marmalade scratch his nose last night?" I was getting a little grumpy, I must admit. Hunter eyed me thoughtfully.

"Come, Surgeon," he said, "I think that perhaps a nice walk in the fresh air is just what the doctor ordered until the night coach arrives."

It is one of Toby Hunter's few faults that he is almost always right.

Chapter Eleven - Thistletongue: master of Law

I felt quite braced and well from a brisk stroll alongside the brook, swishing at the overhanging branches, by the time we came back into the village. Toby had said not much, as usual, but as we came up to the little row of shops, he came more alert and purposeful. "I think it would be very rude of us to depart the village without paying our addresses to one of its most illustrious residents - and his delightful secretary." he said, turning suddenly towards one of the entrances.

The sign over the door - a little less crudely lettered than its neighbours - read 'The Learned Herbert Thistletongue, L.A.' then in smaller type underneath, 'Master of Law - wills prepared, disputes resolved, contracts prepared. Solicitor to the Noble families of Padshire. ' This last advertisement, I imagine, was what had attracted Hunter's attention.

The bell over the door jangled as Toby pressed through, and Miss Lucy Marmalade, a not unattractive pair of pinch-glasses on her nose, looked up first curiously then crossly at us as we came in.

"What do you want?" she exclaimed. "I thought I asked you not to interfere!" But she quickly bit her tongue as her employer heard the noise and shouted out from the back,

"What is it Lucy? I'm trying to concentrate you know!"

Hunter winked at her and strode smartly into the back room before she could move, while I incoherently muttered some apologies.

"Ah, The Learned Mr Thistletongue, L.A., I assume!" Toby roared in his 'friendly' voice. "Delighted to make your acquaintance, sir!" and he bobbed his tail low and nodded his head as deferentially as though the cat had been a Duke.

"Erm - I don't think - have we, er? I don't believe we have met, sir? sirs?" said Thistletongue. He was a mangy old cat, had been quite fully black at one time, but now was greying in his chin and

49

Chapter Eleven - Thistletongue: master of Law

speckled through his fur. His skin hung loosely on his bones as if he had once been very fat, and his shoulder bones poked up nastily like boat-sails as he shifted in his seat. The fur was quite rubbed away and stained blue with ink on his right paw where he was used to scratch a note or hold a pen.

"No, " responded Hunter jovially, "no of course you won't know me, nor my good friend here Robert Twistybones, " I tried not to start at this absurd invention, "but we have a friend in common, I believe, in London - in the legal profession....?" and he paused and smiled broadly.

"Oh! Er - not old Jeremy Hardpads? Why it must be 10 years or more since I saw him? We were at the Law School together as kits you know!"

"Absolutely," Hunter lied, smoothly, "Dear old Jeremy - wanted to send you his very best wishes."

"Did he really? Well how good - fancy him remembering me! And how do you come to...?" Thistletongue looked genuinely pleased - a gleam of happy youthful memory glistened in his eyes. Hunter continued to spin out the most outrageous inventions while we both inspected the office. A large wooden desk, shiny and dark with age, mostly filled the room. It was of the old sort with a sitting-scoop hollowed out deeply on one side, and a counterbalance under a large oil lamp on the other side, filled with lead weights. Big piles of papers, some bound with red or green ribbons and seals occupied both sides of the desk, some typed and some hand-scrawled. Legal books and reference works filled shelves on both sides of the room, and a small stove and kettle behind indicated that strong tea fuelled the great cat's legal works. All my attention was recalled to the present moment though as Thistletongue suddenly called out for Lucy. "Lucy! These fellows know old Jeremy Hardpads! Get us some drinks from the cabinet will you?"

Lucy poked a disapproving nose around the door. "Tea?" she hissed.

Chapter Eleven   Thistletongue: master of Law

"No you silly girl - drinks! I have a nice old bottle of nipjuice in that back cabinet - behind the Archibald dispute papers. Get it, will you? There's some glasses in there too"

"Just the one I think." she muttered, but he seemed not to hear her, nor to notice her slam the door tight behind her once we were all well equipped with warm nipjuice toddies in mugs. I noticed that Hunter merely sniffed at his juice, but once Thistletongue was a good inch into his, Toby turned the subject around to the local legal matters occupying the firm.

"Ah yes, well, you raise an interesting subject, there. It was a very unusual entail, that. Of course I shouldn't speak of it, but it's different between us legal gentlemen I daresay. Matter of professional interest, eh?"

Toby had the delicacy not to respond too directly to this observation, but nodded wisely - he was very interested in legal matters at any rate.

"Yes, yes - very unusual. Old Pinkpaw was very tight with his money - and he didn't think too much of the younger generation. Well it was still pretty new money you see - so he wasn't used to it as the old nobility are." Thistletongue injected a full measure of contempt for the newness of the money into his story - though it seemed he'd been paid a good deal of it. "So he left a good allowance for Lady Corcinda, nothing wrong with that, and money in trust for each of the children, most for Cecil. But he won't get a bean in his own right until his sisters are married off. Sort of like a line of dominoes - each in line can't have anything until the other is safely accounted for. It ensures, you see, that a careless young kit like Cecil can't waste away the capital and diminish the - ahem - great attraction of the estate for potential suitors!"

Hunter indicated with a curled lip his legal contempt for the arrangement. He picked at his teeth with a curled claw, "Something funny about the wedding settlement too wasn't there?

"Thistletongue seemed to fear that he had not provided sufficient astonishment for an audience sent to him by that very great legal entity Jeremy Hardpads. Even so, he clearly felt some embarrassment. "Hem, well, ahem, I don't see how you could have heard about that. And nothing to do with his Lordship that, that was - well that was the Lady Corcinda's doing. Nothing so very odd in that one either. Quite the thing, I hear amongst the nobility these days. Sort of a pre-nuptial agreement. In the event of - well - any future disagreement between Celia and her husband, once they had been married, then she would retain the title, and her capital, less any expenses due for any legal matters. Not very romantic, of course. But then the Greatclaws are known for their dalliances - I suppose that Corcinda is simply trying to look after her stepdaughter's future - and any possible issue... hem. Still I really shouldn't be talking about that."

"No, so you should not, Herbert Thistletongue!" Lucy hissed, banging the door back against the ceiling as she shot into the room. Toby eyed her, thoughtfully, "Ah the delightful Miss Marmalade. Has, perhaps, our coach arrived?"

"It has that, Sir." she returned, calming Thistletongue's wide-eyed alarm with a softer voice. "He's just gone into the King's Head so they'll be ready for the off in half an hour or so."

"Well thank you Miss Marmalade. Very kind, I'm sure. We must be gone, Herbert - the Night Coach waits for no cat. I shall be sure to pass on your best wishes to Jeremiah."

"You mean Jeremy." said Lucy

"Quite so my dear, Judge Jeremy" said Hunter - and compounded his villainy with a further wink.

We made a rapid exit, as Thistletongue sank back behind his piles of papers with a confused and troubled look in his eyes, and Lucy, with pinch-glasses gripping her nose, and paying us pointed inattention, took out her irritation with firm and rapid typing on the writemaker.

Chapter Twelve - some curious letters

5, Brookside Lane
Tangleburr Village
Monday 2nd June

Dear Sir,

I think you will understand my agitation to have seen you in the premises of my employer this afternoon, having made plain to you my *express wish* that you should not interfere in the matter of my brother's demise. As I tried to make clear in our brief meeting, my family and I are indebted to the Pinkpaw family for their kindness to us, and indeed my sister Polly is *still in their employ.* I have no wish to cause them any trouble and indeed I'm sure they deserve none as I am certain that Percy was the victim simply of an unhappy mishap. I have spoken to Polly and *she agrees with me* that it is for the best to leave things as they are and to bury our brother in peace, trying to think the best of him. I beg you, Sir, to do us the courtesy of obeying these wishes.

I am, sir, in all due respect,
yours, sincerely,

Lucy Marmalade. (Miss)

Chapter Twelve - some curious letters

           15, High Street
           Tangleburr Village
           Monday 15th June

Dear Sir,

I was not aware of your profession when we met this weekend past, but have been informed of it since. I consider myself to have been the victim of, at very best, a vicious prank, and at worst an outrageous deception on an articled lawyer. My assistant, whom I have reprimanded severely for her mistake, has admitted to me that she knew your identity when she showed you into my chambers, but omitted to announce you. My mistake, of course, was therefore understandable. But I must enjoin you most severely that you must absolutely not divulge the various confidences which I made to you, whilst under the impression that you were yourself a proper legal personage. I am now not certain whether you are in fact, as you asserted, acquainted with my own old friend Jeremy Hardpaw. I am quite aware that he was something of a trickster in our college days, so perhaps that much was true. I should warn you however, that I intend to write to the Judge myself, to alert him to your bandying of his name.

I am yours, etc

Herbert Thistletongue
Solicitor

Chapter Twelve - some curious letters

....

To TOBY HUNTER of GEORGE STREET

KEEP YOUR NOSE OUT OF WHAT DOES NOT CONCERN YOU OR YOU WILL MEET A BAD ACCIDENT.

A Friend

.....

       Petertail Towers
        Sandyford
         Kent

Dear Sir,
  I have been told by a friend that you can be trusted with a difficult matter requiring great discretion. I hope you can indeed help me - I shall call this Friday afternoon at about 3 o'clock.

   Yours etc
    Lord Petertail

Chapter Twelve - some curious letters

"Well - what do you make of that little lot, eh Robbie?" asked Toby, poking at the fire. It had been nearly a week since our return from Tangleburr village - my practice had occupied me since then but I was free as usual Friday afternoon and had come as is my habit to visit Hunter at his lodgings. A couple of quite interesting medical cases had kept my mind far from the strange business on the Hunt. One very lovely young ladykit had been refusing to eat anything but sardines - having investigated without success her digestion and any possible disorder of the blood, a curious explanation had emerged. It seemed she had fallen in love with a sailor and must be reminded by every meal of the sea! I referred her in the end to a colleague in the new science of psychiatry. But I was instantly excited by this set of Toby's correspondence.

"In order? Well the first is simple - Lucy makes you a plain enough request. I hope you will honour it?"

"Ha! It is simple enough - and I intend honour the promise that I made the girl - not to involve her brother's name in my enquiries. So far I have not done so. But I also made a promise to her sister - to get hold of the cat that caused her brother's death. That I will also do." Hunter gave a particularly savage stab at the fire, and returned to perch on the firestool.

"Hmm - well your enquiries so far then have not helped us so very much. We shall be lucky if the Honourable Judge Hardpaws does not have you in chains according to this second letter!"

Hunter chuckled. "Never fear - as it happens I am indeed - though only slightly - acquainted with Judge Hardpaws. I have in the past given testimony in front of him - in a case where he was only too happy to convict a hardened villain. I have already sent him a note to explain the necessity of the small deception. And I shall set things to rights with Thistletongue, never fear. But you are wrong about the enquiries doing no good - I think we learnt at least two things of very great interest there. And I have applied for a copy of

Chapter Twelve – some curious letters

the original will. We shall see soon for ourselves just how relevant it is."

"Very well then - and this third note - you have annoyed someone with your enquiries. You think it is to do with the same case?"

"That I do, indeed - such charming epistles are not unfamiliar to me - more usual I admit from the rougher sort of villain, whose hand I did not detect here. But did you notice anything strange about it?"

I picked up the note again - it was not, as I had at first thought, typed, but instead formed from words cut from a newspaper, some stuck together from originally different words where the whole had not been readily to hand. "It's all pasted words - from the look of it from a single copy", I said.

"Quite correct - and from which newspaper, do you think? No matter, I can tell you precisely which one - Monday's Times. I found some of the words in an article on the third page. So - an educated correspondent - or at least one that takes the Times for his daily reading…"

"Or has access to it - could be a servant?"

Hunter looked impatient and waved a dismissive paw at me "Tchah - well, perhaps so. But I cannot imagine the ponderous Macintosh sat carefully gumming letters on a page, can you? Besides, consider the notepaper - thick, plain stuff but good quality. And no grammatical errors. This is someone who does not want to be recognised, but I'll hazard someone we have already met. I have no other cases at present of such great significance - it must be the same business."

"Perhaps so - but then will you take the advice of your anonymous friend?" I asked.

"Certainly I should - but I'm afraid the matter does concern me - why two very delightful ladies have separately asked me to investigate the matter!", countered Toby

"And at least one has retracted!"

57

Chapter Twelve - some curious letters

Again, a paw waved this airily away "Pah! So says her sister. I suspect that Lucy Marmalade puts convenient words in her sister's mouth when it suits the cause she deems best for her family. " He looked more grave and stared at me, unblinking, "Believe me, Rob, I would not endanger any of them nor cause them unnecessary trouble. I shall certainly aim to proceed without maligning their brother. But I think he may be a little more closely connected with this matter than we first thought."

"Could this letter be from the same hand as the threatening note to James?"

Toby paused, struck by the thought. "Cerberus take it! Perhaps it could! Pass me that red case, Robbie."

Toby took the letter over to the table under the window, and laid it out flat. He took down a green book from the shelf, and opening it to the back page, slid out the charred remains of the note that had - perhaps - threatened James Greatclaw. He laid it down to the right of the new letter and studied both very closely, his nose almost touching the paper as he sniffed it. He opened the red leather case that I had passed him and took out a small glass tube of fine silver-gray powder and a large fur paintbrush. Toby tipped a little of the powder onto each letter and pushed it around with the brush, blowing the fine powder gently into the corners, then tipped each letter vertically, tapping it gently on the table to tip off the excess. He held each in turn closely up to the light, then laid them down, and swung around in the chair.

"I do not think they have been produced by the same paw. The paper is the same - the same heavy white laid paper, originally cut I think to the same size, though with all the charring it is hard to tell. But that does not signify. One has had letters cut from a newspaper and gummed on. The other has been written by hand. But this time the writer is writing to a detective - they would take more care. However the scent... " he waved the charred letter again under his nose" ... little left, but I think a masculine scent to

Chapter Twelve - some curious letters

this one, while the other..." he spun again and sniffed at the paper. "Rosemary - I could swear to it."

"A female?"

"I believe so. Or a great dandy at least! No simple country cat would wear such a perfume - male or female." Toby waved both letters at me triumphantly "But paw prints, Robbie - we have paw prints! Now make your mark here and pass me that teacup" he indicated an ink pad and some blank paper.

I grumbled that I had no need to send Toby incriminating letters, being quite capable of threatening him to his face if the mood took me, but dabbed my paws in the ink and made two marks on the paper while Toby dabbed his print powder onto the teacup.

"Celia's." He explained while he worked... " I thought I had better keep it for purposes of elimination. But I had quite forgotten about it until now." He examined the letters again, glancing to and fro from the papers to my prints and those on the teacup.

"Well your greasy paws have made a mess of most of those around the edge, but I can still make out Celia's fine hand here, next to the word 'danger'.. There is one other set of prints that I do not know, but it is probably James. So nothing there. And on the other... nothing. " He cast the papers down again, crossly.

"These scandal sheets do detectives no favours to publicise every advance in criminology - every school miss knows now about paw prints. Tchah."

I tried to shake him out of his mood.

"And what of this other letter? That does sound new - and intriguing."

"So it does, doesn't it?" retorted Toby with a sly grin, "Well we shall see what this gentleman has to say soon enough", and he pointed his tail at the mantel clock, just now nearing 3 in the afternoon.

At that moment I heard a small town carriage rattle up to the door, and jumped up to observe a very sleek brown furred young cat in a wide brimmed bowler hat approach the door. Mrs Neatwhisker let

Chapter Twelve - some curious letters

him in, and Toby and I jumped to our seats, I snatching up a newspaper, and he a copy of Pooters' as our guest tramped up the stairs.

Chapter Thirteen - the missing diamond

Our visitor, a sleek Burmese, doffed his hat and without ceremony made himself comfortable, lighting, with a coal from the fire, a small cigar he had extracted from his hatband.
Toby wrinkled his nose with irritation - he never smoked. "Lord Petertail, I presume?" he said, dipping his tail.
"S'right, old boy - no need for the formalities. Call me Peter - all the chaps do. I say, do you have an ashtray?"
"No - I do not generally smoke - and nor generally do my guests in these rooms" replied Hunter, with a sniff.
"Oh well not to worry - I'm close enough to the grate," said Petertail, tapping his cigar ash in the fire. Subtleties were evidently quite in vain here! "S'pose you're Hunter, then? Who's that fellow?"
"That fellow is my very good friend Surgeon Robert Gentlepaw. You may speak quite freely in front of him. He sometimes documents my cases or assists in medical matters. How may I assist you?"
Lord Peter Petertail was a handsome cat, with sleek dark brown fur, and brilliant blue eyes. He was generally quite slim, though tending a little to fat around his middle. His looks were sadly let down by his manner, which was louche, lazy and condescending. He looked around the room, remarking on its comfort.
Toby's chambers were indeed very comfortable. A small green leather sofa, worn soft with age, sat opposite the grate where a small fire burned hot in winter. In summer Mrs Neatwhisker would fill jars with blooms from the garden - today white hydrangeas. A stiff, high backed armchair sat in a corner to the right of the window which overlooked the back yard, and stuffed bookshelves filled the wall either side of the chimney breast. Plump firestools sat in front of the grate, and an ancient wooden chest, bound in metal, with hinges rusted shut sat between the sofa

Chapter Thirteen - the missing diamond

and the fire. Under the window, a polished oak desk was crammed in, slightly blocking the full opening of the door. Indeed, the overwhelming impression of the room was fullness. Mrs Neatwhisker generally managed to keep it in order, but at the end of a weekend without her tidying, Hunter would cover every flat surface with newspapers, books, ink and crumbs, and it would be impossible to move from one corner of the room to another without treading on some vital paper. Our guest sat in corner armchair, puffing on a cigar.

"Righto then - well bit of a tricky thing - I've been seeing this girl, you see. Tremendous, she is - very lovely. Very talented. Mama don't approve, my mama, that is. And - well, wanted to take her to dinner, somewhere a bit special - so we went out to Mitzy's last week. And - um. Well one minute it was there, next it wasn't - you see?" And Petertail took another puff at his cigar, confident that this tale explained the matter in full.

"I'm afraid I don't, Lord Peter - what was missing?"

"Well the Petertail diamond! Dreadful thing - been in the family since - well who knows, really. Forever. Haven't dared tell mama yet - so she - someone suggested you could find it. Sort it out see? I can pay you - got my allowance today. Want to know if it's Gertie, too - hope not. But best to know, ain't it."

Toby hissed quietly in frustration. "Are you telling me, Lord Peter, that you allowed your - friend - to wear the Petertail Diamond out to dinner at Mitzy's restaurant? And that it was stolen from her person?"

"Precisely! now how much will you need?"

"I imagine that to know the answer to that question you should consult the ransom note." tutted Toby.

"What note? I didn't get any note! Been racking my brains what to do ..." Peter retorted

"Yes, well I suspect your robbers will have been waiting for your allowance to be due. You have lodgings in town?"

"Yes - 34, Gloucester Road."

Chapter Thirteen - the missing diamond

"I recommend that you return there at once and check the post - no doubt there will be a note. Once you have it bring it back to me and I will be able to advise you."

"I say do you really think so? Good stuff! Best just to pay up you think?"

Toby's claws were dug firmly into the firestool. "No, that is not what I said. If you pay immediately you may not recover the diamond and there are likely to be further demands. Bring me the note and we will consider how best to proceed."

"Ha. Stout fellow - clever thinking, that. And what about Gertie? Fellow don't liked to be fooled you know. Will you find out if she's 'in on it'?" Petertail cast the stub of his cigar into the grate and examined his claws in an embarrassed manner.

"It seems highly likely that she is involved. But you had better give me the full facts," said Hunter.

"Full?"

"Well for a start what is this delightful lady's name? And profession? You said she was - talented?"

A dreamy expression crossed Petertail's face. "Gertie I call her. 'Cause her real name is Gertrude Fluff. Funny name, eh? But you'd know her as Georgina Blackeyes"

Suddenly Petertail had our full attention. Hunter looked quite astonished. I was quite astonished. Georgina Blackeyes had been the toast of the theatrical world for some three years now. Her beautiful face adorned the society pages of every other weekend supplement - and occasional advertisements for clawcreams and furwash. She was currently appearing, as I recalled, in a popular production of some farcical comedy at the Savoy theatre. I had read that her admirers included some of the aristocatcy but had not particularly recalled Petertail's name - he seemed in any case a little young for the lady. I had always fancied that a more mature, reliable sort of cat would win her heart.

"Georgina Blackeyes - the actress?" I gasped.

Chapter Thirteen - the missing diamond

"Gertie. Yes - though she hates me calling her that in public. Says it's not her 'image'.

This was considerably more interesting. Although surely not rich enough to afford the Petertail diamond, Georgina Blackeyes was a huge success. She could have no need to steal. Hunter hunched forward in concentration. "What...what, precisely occurred that evening, Lord Petertail?" Tell us in detail from the moment you handed over the diamond."

"Ha ha! The detective at work, eh? Right, well, I knew that mama was going to be out. And where she kept the thing. Always showing it off at parties y'see? And Gertie loves jewels. So, special treat, I'd told her she could wear it."

"She was aware of this before that evening."

"Yes, I'd promised her - it was her birthday."

"I see, go on" said Hunter, scribbling a note on a small pad.

"Well I got it out of the case alright, and Gertie put it on. It's on a black silk ribbon. Or it was anyway. It looked beautiful, sparkling away against her black fur...."

"We don't need to know that! What happened then? Any incidents on the way to the restaurant? Was the diamond out of your sight at all?"

"No, not once! We got a carriage straight there. Doorman showed us to the best table. And it was a terrific meal. Top drawer. And Gertie looking marvellous. Happiest cat in the room I was" Petertail licked his lips in appreciative memory. "And then the next minute it was just gone! "

"Precisely when?"

"After our coffee arrived. I'd spilled mine, oaf that I am, and Gertie was dabbing at the cloth. And when we'd both sat up again she noticed it was gone. Quite a scream she has!"

"You had coffee? Who ordered it?"

"Well I don't see what that has to do with it. I did all the ordering - but I know that Gertie always has coffee."

Chapter Thirteen - the missing diamond

Hunter's eyes narrowed "And I suppose the waiter rushed over, when you spilt the coffee?"

"Yes - but that can't have been it. Gertie started screaming before he got there." Petertail looked anxious." I say this is thirsty work, investigating - do you have anything to drink?" Hunter nodded at me and I extracted a small bottle of ancient honeysuckle sherry from the cupboard, which was kept in reserve for more anxious or upset clients.

Petertail supped noisily on the glass. "Not bad, this - what is it? Yes, so there it was, anyway. Gone! And neither of us with any idea where it had gone to! Or so she swears. I - I had her bag searched, you know. Not sure she'll forgive me for that. "

I was appalled. "You had Georgina Blackeyes searched? For a stolen diamond! In the middle of Mitzy's restaurant?! Good Bast!"

"No, no! I ain't a fool, Cerberus take you! " No - the management were very understanding. They know me there and - well sometimes a fellow has a bit of trouble with a girl. They're used to that. Saw it was difficult. So they offered to search. Very diplomatic. Suggested the clasp might have broken off - could have fallen into her bag. But it wasn't there."

"I imagine Miss Blackeyes was not impressed. But she consented to the search?" asked Hunter

"Well - yes. Sort of sneered at me while they looked though."

"I imagine so! And you had not lost sight of Miss Blackeyes - or the diamond - not for a moment between abstracting it from your mother's room, and the moment it disappeared?" Hunter was insistent - he clearly had some idea.

"No. Well she went to powder her nose, you know, when we arrived. But she was wearing it when she came back to the table. She remarked then on how it caught the light."

Hunter sat back, pleased. "I see. Well I think we can help you, Lord Peter. But we will need that note and - I think it will take a few days. When is your mama due back?"

Chapter Thirteen - the missing diamond

"Next Friday! Oh Bast! You simply must get it back before then, Mr Hunter - she'll... oh she always always checks on it as soon as she's home. Can you get it?"

Hunter picked at a loose thread on the firestool, "Oh I think so, Lord Peter - but I can make you no promises at present. Send me the note when it arrives and we'll be in touch."

Chapter Fourteen - Mitzy's

Toby clearly had some good idea what had happened to the diamond, but utterly refused to give me a clue, merely chuckling to himself and promising me "a good night's entertainment". And he bade me locate my opera-cloak!
My friend rarely mistook himself, so I took him at his word, and returned to George Street some hours later, top-hat, white tie and cloak firmly secured. I generally think a cat looks a bit of a fool in a top-hat, but an opera-cloak looks more ridiculous in isolation. And I'll admit I was somewhat looking forward to meeting the fabulous Georgina Blackeyes, for I was certain that was what Toby had in mind. He met me at the porch, with his topper somehow at the perfect angle to convey a casual style. "Well, Robbie - ready to meet gorgeous Georgina?" he chuckled, poking a cane at a small flower poking out of my pocket.
"Hadn't considered it. Seemed only polite to take the great actress a bokay." I grumbled.
"Indeed it is, Rob, very thoughtful of you. But I fear your flowers will wilt away in your pocket - we are going to Mitzy's first."
I cheered up immediately. Mitzy's is of course the absolute top place to go in town at present, though I do not generally allow such an indulgence for myself unless very fully in funds. It was indeed promising to be quite a special evening. "I'll get the cab" I purred.
"No need, old chap - I thought we'd get the train. " said Toby, his eyes glittering. "Come along, we don't want to miss it. "
We strolled down the hill towards the station. I should have guessed that Toby would want to use this excuse to try the new steaming-train carriage. I was still not keen on the things, preferring to rely on dog-cabs or horse carts, but he loved anything new and mechanical. We queued with the mix of the curious and idle at the ticket-window. I endured some mild mockery of my

outfit, while I waited for the station-cat to stamp a thick card billet with the date, then boarded the train.

Thick puffs of steam blasted from its chimney as the steam-maker piled firebricks into the cabin furnace. The contraption seemed coiled, like a skittish horse and I clung grimly to the leather strap by the window awaiting the off. Toby was skittish himself, clambering all over the carriage and poking his head out of the window, twitching with excitement. "What a wonderful machine it is! There's no end to what could be done with these engines! Why it could replace all the carriages of the road!" he cried.

"Hardly so while ladies still wish to travel." I retorted.

"Not so, for there are two ladies boarding just now! But perhaps the dog carriage will still be required for old-fashioned medical men of a nervous disposition?"

Sadly I could not give this inanity the rejoinder it required, my heart filling my mouth as we jolted out of the station. Indeed the trip was somewhat smoother than I had feared, and I managed to let go the leather strap in several places on the way. However I kept my eyes firmly fixed ahead, on the curve of the track and the puffs of steam, while Toby gaped at London flying past at incredible speed.

The one great advantage of the steaming train carriage is its speed, and we were soon at Charing Cross station. I wondered for the thousandth time what the Charing Cross could possibly have been - there has never been a trace of one found there. Mitzy's was just to the south in the park overlooking the river. An exceedingly glossy black cat took our cloaks and hats. All of Mitzy's front of house staff have coats of purest black or white, matching the chequered floor of the restaurant itself. We were shown to a corner table. It was not the best, which was the centre table occupied by a prominent politician and his family, but we had a good view of it.

Chapter Fourteen - Mitzy's

"Perfect" muttered Toby, sipping on his frothed milk cocktail, " do you see, Robbie - they have not long sat down. We shall study the whole thing."

I had been hoping to do rather more studying of Mitzy's marvellous menu, and hurriedly selected a starter. Our neighbours were doing the same, but the waiter approached them first. We could not hear their conversation, but saw them pointing out items they had chosen, and his dutiful nodding, accompanied by the occasional thumbscratch in a waiters' grid. He left their table and came straight to ours. "You order, " Toby hissed, his gaze still intent on the centre table.

I gladly obliged, delighted that I need not make a firm choice between two favourite fish courses until they arrived, then the waiter swished out towards the kitchens at the back. A second waiter was approaching the centre table with their starters. They looked spectacular. On one plate, great King Prawns swam on a bed of oystergreen, trapped under a cobweb net of spun sugarglass. On another I spied sardines, somehow leaping as if suspended in the air over a quivering hens' egg yolk. The young kittens at the centre table squeaked excitedly, until batted quiet by their mother, who attempted to look unmoved.

I am quite ashamed to report that after this, as our own meal began to arrive, I paid even less attention to the neighbouring table and more and more to my own plate. Mitzy's fully lived up to its reputation, and I intended to do it justice. Toby meanwhile, picked idly at dish after dish until the family beside us left, even the kittens quieted by the stupendous meal. I was licking happily at a cream ice as the wait-staff began to clear and clean their table. "Well?" Toby's gaze caught mine. "You saw it?"

"Herr-umph. Ah - well I saw - I say what did you think of those little chicken wotsits on sticks?"

"Never mind the chicken!" Toby barked, "You saw the sequence, on the other table."

Chapter Fourteen - Mitzy's

"Ah, well I think I saw some of it - bit distracted." I dabbed a paw hopefully at the bowl. There was none left. "Run me through it?"
"Tchah! Two waiters serve the table - one takes the orders for each course, he's pure black fur, the other in white fur serves. You can clearly see them arrive, and leave. They go in and out of that swing-door in the kitchen to the right of the entrance." As Toby gestured, I could see the tail of one waiter disappear into the kitchen, just evading the swinging door. "So the order-taker visits the table five times, once to take orders for firsts and mains, once for dessert, once to check on the table, twice to deliver and then to collect the bill. The server more often to deliver all the food, and clear the plates. "
"So? You'd still notice if one of them snatched a great big diamond along with the soup-bowl!"
Toby laughed uproriously, to the disapproval of our fellow diners, in hushed reverence of Mitzy's best. "Right you are Robbie - so how was it done?"
"Well - the coffee, wasn't it? Petertail spilled his coffee, there's a bit of a fuss, and then - "
"Yes? What then? A waiter comes over to clean up - but his attention is on Petertail, and vice versa. Lord Peter would surely have noticed the waiter breaking off to snatch the diamond from his companion. Think, Robbie - who is unobserved?"
"Well, Georgina - but it can't have been her!"
"Why not?
"Well she's the most marvellous actress - those eyes!"
"Surely an advantage - to act surprised, outraged, and all the time..."
"But she didn't have it! The cad had her searched - there was nothing on her."
"Perhaps so - let us see. Oh sir?" Toby attracted our waiter with an extended claw.
"Sir - enjoyed the meal? " asked our waiter with an alarmed look at Toby's half toyed-with cream-ice.

Chapter Fourteen · Mitzy's

"Oh yes, very nice. Now I have a question for you - about a little trouble here two nights ago. "

"There is no - trouble - at Mitzy's " hissed the waiter. "Sir must have mistaken the place."

"Oh I think not. " smiled Toby. " A friend of mine, Lord Petertail - had a little accident with a family heirloom - and a lady friend."

"Ah! I think I recollect - a small misunderstanding. Sir understands, the Lord he was - he had enjoyed very much his evening. He was quite excitable. He had some confusion I think. "

"The lady was - understanding?" Toby stared hard at the waiter, whose exotic accent faltered slightly.

"Miss Blackeyes is a very good customer here - very often she is here with admirers. But the Petertails - we cannot afford to upset the nobility, you see?"

"Yes, I think I see that"

"So we conducted - a small search. Very discreet. After all there was not much to see. She had the very tiny pawbag. But there was nothing."

"She was angry?"

"Eh - amused almost. She is quite the lady. Too good for him. You are the detectives?"

"I am Toby Hunter, this is my good colleague Surgeon Gentlepaw. One more question, if you please - did the Lady return?"

"Detectives indeed sir! Yes, I cannot imagine how you guess it - she come back, perhaps 2 hours later- we were about to close. She had left a comb, she thought. An unfortunate evening!"

"She found it?"

"Yes, I think so - she said it was dropped in the toilettes. I assure you, there was no theft here. Lord Peter - was drunk."

And with this very un-Mitzy like statement our waiter returned to address himself to the new occupants of the centre table.

"Could that be it? Lord Peter was tipsy?" I pondered.

Chapter Fourteen - Mitzy's

"Hardly - however bubbled he was, Lord Petertail could hardly invent the presence at the table of the famous Petertail diamond."

Chapter Fifteen - The Savoy Theatre

The great Savoy Theatre is, as I am sure you will know, one of the most popular of London's theatres. It is famed both for the quality of its productions, and the beauty of its interior, almost all preserved in original Yooman style. Of course additional cushions are required on the seats to enhance their comfort and ensure a decent view!

Hunter had obtained - how I cannot imagine - seats of the first quality, in a small elegant box to the left of the stage, from which we would have a superb view of the show. I enjoyed the play somewhat - a version as I recall of Tibbles' "Much Yowl about Nothing", though in modern costume. I must admit that I was overcome by a post-supper snooze and missed something of the second half. However my sixth sense was surely quite alert, for I sneezed awake in the final scene, to observe the marvellous Georgina Blackeyes, actual tears quivering in her dark liquid eyes, declaiming her innocence alternately to her accuser - and to the balcony. All ended well of course (I hope I don't spoil the plot for you - you should certainly see the play!) and I whistled and stomped my feet soundly in approval. Toby held me still, however, as the crowd, having assured the cast of their enjoyment with three curtain-calls, began to disperse.

"What did you think of her performance, Robbie? The bit you weren't snoring through that is?"

"Nonsense, Hunter, didn't miss a thing!" I was confident in this small deception for I certainly do not snore. "Oh she's very good, isn't she. Really very good. I was quite afraid for her when that villain threatened her with the sword in the first scene."

"And the play? What about the section with the crocodile? I thought it an unnecessary modern spoiling of a classic."

I'd seen too many of Hunter's interrogation tricks to fall for this childish nonsense.

Chapter Fifteen - The Savoy Theatre

"Tchah! Crocodile - what nonsense - you're the one who's been asleep, detective! Play was perfectly acceptable. Though I agree I prefer the more classic versions. Strange to have them all traipsing about in modern hats and capes."

Hunter gave me a wry smile. "Well we shall ask the opinion of the great lady herself. I happened to do a small favour once for the proprietor of this theatre, and he has agreed to allow a great fan backstage for an audience."

My throat dried. It is not every day that one gets to meet ones heroes. Let alone the more attractive of them. I nervously patted the posy in my pocket - it had largely crumbled to bits but something might be salvaged. The theatre had mainly cleared, save one or two gentlecats who were indeed quite soundly asleep, and being shaken awake by the cleaners. Though I did think that I saw Lady Corcinda, opera-glasses to her nose, huddled in the corner of an upper box. No doubt my eyes or the remnants of sleep deceived me, for I cannot conceive of that Grand country lady as an habitué of the theatre. We walked down to the entrance hall and were accompanied by the manager to a small row of doors in a gloomy corridor behind the stage, the last of which was marked with a golden rose. He scraped lightly on the door , "Madame, those admirers of yours that I mentioned, they are here."

The voice I had already heard that evening in tones of both despair and delight sang out from behind the door, "One moment please, Alfred, I am not quite ready".

I pulled the posy from my pocket, trying to shield it slightly from Alfred's view. It was mostly useless, but a single pink rose, still mainly in bud, looked acceptable. I kicked the remnants to one side, then looked up sharply to see the door open wide, and a complete vision of loveliness filled my view. Georgina's great expressive eyes were very unusually dark, almost black in colour, so that they seemed big enough to drown in. They had the trick also of appearing permanently moist with emotion of one kind or another. I was immediately convinced upon seeing her face so close, that this lady could commit no crime, but that she could certainly command my protection, if she would but ask it. I wordlessly offered my wilted rose. She was charm itself, "Oh but how elegant, how thoughtful! What a true gentlecat you have brought to me, Alfred. You see, he is not like these mindless brutes with their armfuls of lilies - a single delicate rose. Because he can see that I am a lone and delicate flower. Do come in, welcome, gentlecats."

The dressing room was small, but beautifully furnished to suit a lady. The walls were plainly whitewashed, and a small pale gray dressing table, awash with delicate trinkets and mysterious ointments was pressed against the left wall. A tea tray, with flowery teapot, cups, cream jug and a full bowl of sugar lumps topped a small round tea stand. A dainty chair, plump with pink velvet cushions sat in the opposite corner, and a delicate floral scent filled the air. Georgina jumped up on the cushioned chair and curled herself elegantly.

We sat in front of her.

"You enjoyed the play?" purred Georgina. Her very voice seemed plush with velvet tones.

I gurgled hopelessly, so Toby answered for us both. "Oh indeed, my dear lady, a very interesting and modern interpretation. And I must express my admiration for your artistry. Most convincing, especially when in peril."

Georgina narrowed her eyes, "Well but of course, Mr Hunter, I am an actress!"

"Of course. Indeed we were discussing your talents in that direction only yesterday with a mutual acquaintance."

"Who do you mean?" she uncurled and moved to the tea-tray. "Tea? It is Russian 'chay'. It must be drunk neat - without cream, sugar. Very elegant"

"Why not, madame. Yes, your friend the noble Lord Petertail. I believe he was witness to quite a unique performance - at Mitzy's."

Chapter Fifteen - The Savoy Theatre

Georgina halted in her pouring of the rather weak-looking tea. She laughed, a delightful tinkling laugh.

"Really! That - Petertail is no longer a friend of mine. He made quite a fool of himself. Having insisted - quite insisted, mind - that I must join him for dinner. And at Mitzy's - so who am I to refuse? He makes the outrageous suggestion that I had stolen - stolen mind you - some family heirloom. Such nonsense. He was quite drunk, hardly the gentlecat and he gave me the thing in the first place. But he made the most embarrassing scene at Mitzy's. My favourite restaurant and I hardly dare show my face."

"And yet you did show your face - almost immediately."

Georgina passed me a cup of the Russian 'chay', and smiled, as weakly as the tea.

"I had lost a comb."

"May I see it?"

"No. I think perhaps you had better leave, Mr Hunter. My admirers do not usually ask such rude questions."

"Oh we shall leave - Gertie - but I do not think we shall leave without that diamond."

"Well that's where you're wrong then - because I don't have it."

Imperceptibly, as she spoke, Georgina's manner had coarsened, and her eyes, though still dark brown, seemed more and more ordinary in size, and harder in nature.

Hunter smiled slowly and paced towards her, "Are you quite certain my dear - you know I think I cannot quite drink this tea without sugar after all?" and saying this he snatched up the sugar bowl. Georgina flew at him, lashing out wildly with her claws, but he had already dashed the bowl to the floor. A sudden blaze of light seemed to flare up from the amongst the broken shards of china, and Toby plucked up the stone. It was the Petertail diamond.

I came at last to my senses, and managed somehow to restrain the furious Georgina - Gertie, perhaps I should say, for she was

Chapter Fifteen The Savoy Theatre

assailing both our ears with the most vicious and unpleasant threats, sauced with thoroughly unladylike swearing! We were interrupted by a hammering at the door - Alfred, checking on his charge. "Everything alright Georgina?"

Hunter placed a paw in front of her mouth and whispered urgently in her ear "Tell him you're fine if you don't want a scandal." Gertie, her fur ruffled, struggled briefly with her fury then heaved a sigh and relaxed in my grip. She sang out, in the same beautiful tones in which she had greeted us, "Oh certainly, Alfred, the silly gentlecats managed to knock over my teastand - no harm done!" Alfred padded away and Toby signalled to me to let Gertie go. She paced furiously, still cursing lightly under her breath. Hunter turned the gemstone under the candlelight. It was enormous, perhaps the size and roughly the shape of a small hen's egg, and sparkled from every one of a hundred facets. A shaft of light caught on Gertie's eyes, and she hissed at Toby, "Well, what do you want? You have it now, why don't you go?"

"Some information, I think, first of all. You met Petertail quite accidentally?"

Gertie looked scornful, "I meet who I want to meet. There's plenty of foolish young aristocrats like to annoy their mamas by dining with an actress. I am famous you know."

"And rightly so, I should say," observed Hunter, "your performance is usually flawless. So you had him in mind as a victim - you had heard, I presume of the Petertail diamond."

Gertie's face softened as she looked at the diamond, still twirling and teasing the candlelight in Hunter's paws. "It's the biggest egg-diamond in London. I wanted it."

"Another one for the collection, I assume. This is not the first mysterious jewel-theft this season. How could you hope to keep getting away with it?"

"Toms are fools, that's how." sniffed Gertie. "I've generally taken little the Mamas would miss - or not quickly. And the young idiots don't like to think they've been gulled. So they don't admit it.

Chapter Fifteen - The Savoy Theatre

Replace the trinket somehow out of their allowances, or out of paste." She smiled - and Hunter returned her smile.

"Very well then, you have afforded my friend and I a very pleasant few days diversion. For which I thank you." Gertie offered a mocking actor's bow. "But I think perhaps it is time that you considered your jewellery collection complete. And you might find that you have tired of London."

Gertie contemplated her claws. "Well I must complete the run first." She shot Toby a shrewd look, " I don't sell any of it - I just like the gems. So I must still earn my living. Still, perhaps a tour of the provinces might be fun."

"No doubt you would find it entertaining - as well as your audiences!" returned Toby with a grin.

"Your friend don't say much." observed Gertie, as we turned to go.

"No, I fear he is often thunderstruck by beautiful ladies. And by fallen idols. Come, Robbie, we must leave Miss Blackeyes to her toilette."

And so we left the theatre, pausing only to be half crushed in the corridor by two stage-hands, wrestling with a large stuffed crocodile.

Chapter Sixteen - The Hen's egg returned.

Toby had summoned Petertail to his chambers for three o clock the following day. But he had promised me first - in response to the appalled entreaties I had made on regaining my composure - to explain all.

"It was evident to me from the first that Miss Blackeyes was our thief. But I could not be sure how she had effected the seizure until we dined at Mitzy's. You recall our researches there?"

I mainly recalled an excellent supper before my digestion was disturbed by shock, but nodded assent.

"Well as you observed yourself, it was clear that no waiter or diner could have snatched the diamond from the table without being noticed unless there was some disturbance. Even then, there was nowhere to put it. The plates were taken away rapidly, the floor was solid and hardly a safe place to leave it. It was not in Georgina's bag, which was thoroughly searched in front of Peter. Where could it have gone?"

"The.. sugarbowl?" Hunter patted my shoulder gently. "I thought of that at first - indeed it immediately struck me as the obvious place she would have kept the diamond in her dressing room until she could hide it more permanently. But no, not at Mitzy's. Think - they were both taken away from the table immediately after the gem disappeared. She would have had no chance to retrieve it; she did not come back for hours and even then what could be her excuse to search the sugarbowls? What else was on the table?"

"Well nothing - plates, forks and coffee cups."

"Very nearly right, Robbie, coffee cups, yes - full of coffee."

"She dropped it in the coffee?"

"She did indeed."

"But that's useless too, surely. She could not have retrieved that either."

Chapter Sixteen - The Hen's egg returned.

"No, she could not - and nor could anyone else. I imagine it dissolved quite quickly - the coffee was still pretty hot."
"Dissolved? What are you talking about?" I was getting quite cross. There are explanations and there is riddling.
"It was paste - sugar paste."
"No it wasn't. You've got it there - solid as anything!"
"This, Robbie, is the Petertail diamond." Hunter expounded in a lecturing tone whilst batting the gemstone back and forth to himself on the table. "This little trinket was hidden snugly in the ladies' powder room for retrieval at a convenient moment. Though Georgina did not dare wait beyond a few hours. No, the paste substitute which she brought with her in her purse and wore back to the table was the one she dissolved in the coffee. Pity, for it must have been remarkably fine workmanship to fool Lord Petertail for even an hour. Ah - I think I hear the bell."

Lord Peter Petertail did not seem in the mood to be announced, for I hear the unmistakeable noise of an irritated housekeeper mingled with the rapid pad of his feet on the stairs. He pushed into the room and sprawled on a seat. "Well? Do you have it? There was never any note. Please say that you have it, Mama returns today!"
"Ah Lord Petertail, would you care for some tea? You seem somewhat agitated."
"Agitated! I should say so! Mama's back today I tell you! I can't replace the damn thing - she'll.. oh Bast if she won't stop my allowance."
"You should really take some tea, it's very good. And the only thing to go with Mrs Neatwhisker's seed cake. Yes, I think I can encourage you that we have made some progress. Your Miss Blackeyes was not able to help us, unfortunately..."
I pricked my whiskers at this deception, but no doubt Hunter had his reasons.
"...but we were nonetheless able to locate the diamond."

Chapter Sixteen   The Hen's egg returned.

Petertail slumped on the chair and whistled slowly. "It wasn't my Gertie then? Strange, I was half sure it was. That's no good anymore, though. She's leaving town anyway it seems. The play's going on tour. And she won't answer my messages. Can't blame her, I s'pose. Must have been one of those oily foreign waiters then. No, don't worry, I know you detectives have your code, I needn't know how you found it. But just please I must have it - I have to get it back into the safe before six tonight." He finally accepted the offered cup, then immediately dropped it with a yowl as if it was burning hot. The Petertail diamond rolled lazily in the smashed china.

"Forgive me the amateur dramatics," drawled Toby, "it seemed appropriate to the case."

But Peter was already dancing delighted around the room. "Oh you marvel, Hunter. Superb stuff! She'll never know. Ha ha! You must send me your bill! I shall double it!"

"Don't speak too soon." I muttered, for Toby had a habit of charging clients in proportion to the degree of annoyance they caused him.

But Toby was laughing at Peter's antics and brushed the offer aside. "I could not accept it - a recommendation to your friends will do. The case has been a very pleasant diversion."

"Consider it done already, old chap. Though you don't need recommending in many circles. I got your name from the most impeccable source."

"Really? And who was this source?"

"A Kitduke, no less! " bragged Peter, lighting a cigar. "The Kitduke Julius Greatclaw." And slipping the diamond carefully into his pocket, he bounced out of the room.

We were both silent for a moment. I gingerly began to collect the smashed pieces of cup. "Mrs N won't thank you for this. " I grumbled. "That's her favourite china you know."

Chapter Sixteen - The Hen's egg returned.

"Blast the china!" cursed Toby. "I've been fooled, Robert - taken for a blasted fool!" He was furious, clawing at the couch in frustration. "They knew warnings wouldn't work so they gave me a toy to play with. And I danced for them like a puppet. Tchah!"
"Danced? For who? It is very curious that Greatclaw should commend you to Petertail after he was so abrupt. But surely there is no more to it than that. Do calm yourself Toby and stop clawing at the furniture!"
Toby hissed slowly and drew a calmer breath. "You are right, Robbie, though I fear not about the purpose of the recommendation. I said myself it was diverting, did I not? I'll wager you there are a dozen similar fool's errands in that pile of unopened post, noble Kits and Misses with all manner of trivial mishaps, recommended to my discreet and insightful attention by the kindly Julius. Tch! Well no more distractions. We must get back to the case! What is the urgency here? What event are we being distracted from?"
Toby snatched up the newspaper, riffling urgently through the announcements at the back. "Ha!" he shouted, "I have it - but oh my dear Robert, we have very little time."
I took the paper from his hand, a circle was scratched around the following notice:

"It is the <u>great pleasure</u> of the Lady Corcinda Pinkpaw, relict of the late Lord Charles Pinkpaw, to announce the wedding of her step-daughter, Milady Celia, to the Honourable KitDuke Julius Greatclaw, son of the noble Duke Gregory Greatclaw of Clawcastle. The <u>wedding</u> will take place on the 30th August in the Great Western Chapel in London."

Chapter Seventeen - Family trees.

The newspaper fell to the floor - Toby's eyes were thin and troubled. "Why,"I said, "that's still nearly a month off. We surely still have time to catch our attempted murderer. If you believe there was such a person?"
"Oh most surely there was" snapped Hunter, grimly, " - and murderer, not attempted only. For if you recall, surgeon, a cat did die, even if it was not the cat intended. Good Bast, what have I been doing? Robbie, fetch your notes, we must review what we know of the case and decide our next move."
I fetched out my case notes from my medical bag and flicked back to the date of Celia's first visit to George Street. "I have it all here, Toby. Where should I begin?"
"At the beginning, of course. " said Toby, jumping up to the firestool and closing his eyes in concentration.
"Celia's first visit?"
"No!" he rejoined sharply, " No - this case begins much longer ago. With three noble families and their intentions for their descendants. Let us begin with the noble Lords Pinkpaw and Greatclaw, some thirty years ago."
"Well we don't know much about that!"
"True, we know very little, but we can guess at much."
I flicked through my scratched notes for anything of use, and searched my memory as well. "Lord Charles Pinkpaw - he was a seed merchant. Or came from a family in that trade at any rate. They were wealthy, but not of a very long noble line. He married Lady Corcinda Sharpclaw...."
Toby hissed to me to stop. "Ah, but that was his second marriage, was it not? There was already a kitten from the first - Celia."
"Hum - well, yes, I suppose so. We know that Lady Corcinda describes her as a step-daughter."
"And what happened to this first wife?"

Chapter Seventeen - Family trees.

"Nobody seems to know"

"Not even the omniscient Pooter?" Toby leapt up from the chair to snatch the volume from the bookshelf. He threw it down to me and I turned to the pages about the Pinkpaws.

"Here - it reads:

Pinkpaw, Lord Charles - Charles was the third Lord Pinkpaw, inheritor of the noble title from his father, the noted gentlecat of the remote Highoak manor, Nottingham. The original Lord Pinkpaw was so ennobled by our great King Henry V in recognition of his services to the army during the war with France....."

"Supplying fly-blown biscuits, no doubt!" tutted Toby.

"...before the death of his own father, when Charles was still KitLord, his first wife, Milady Maria Pinkpaw nee Muddlenose, died in kitbirth, and was survived by only Milady Celia Pinkpaw, of Talltrees Kent. He shortly thereafter married Milady Corcinda Pinkpaw nee Sharpclaws, who later had issue Cecil and Lillia. Charles relocated the family to Talltrees Kent on his accession to the title and Highoak manor is now let to the Bluefurs of Nottingham. Lord Charles died last year of a stroke. " I stopped - "That's all that Pooters has to say on Charles.

"Unusual, but nothing to point to there. So just one kitten survived and the mother did not. But it happens. We have also the rumours of violence against Lady Corcinda. Just how 'shortly' thereafter did they marry, I wonder. And why did he leave Nottingham?"

"Perhaps he wanted to be closer to the capital? The theatre, gambling?"

"Actresses, perhaps - there were rumours of that too. And what of the Greatclaws?"

"Who has not heard of the Greatclaws? There are statue to both General Hardclaws atop his pony and Duke Greatwhisker waving a sword in Parliament Square! The union of those two great families began the Greatclaw line some hundred years ago."

"And recently?" Toby idly scratched letters in the mantelpiece - C - S - C - P - J - G ....

I turned back to Pooters. "Kitduke Julius Greatclaw and his brother Harry are the two eldest kits of Duke Gregory Greatclaw. Their mother the Duchess Ammelia Greatclaw also bore one other boy, James and three girls, Melia, Jania and Amy. They reside in the Claw Castle at the centre of the family estate in Kent, and during the season in their townhouse in Kensington."

"What about money?"

"Well you cannot expect Pooters to remark on that!"

"Indeed, no - but the rumour is rife in London that they have none. Ten generations of excess, falling rents, gambling and large families - no doubt they are wondering where three dowries will come from for those girls."

"And so - Celia...?"

"I doubt it is as calculating as all that. Celia is a beauty, and Julius' mama no doubt gave him licence to choose a love-match from amongst any of the nobility, provided that his beloved could restore the family fortunes without disgrace to the name that ,is! Pah! This is no good - all this is well known. What have we discovered that we could not read in any fashion magazine?" Toby snatched up the newspaper again. "The marriage is to proceed in a month. Think, Robbie - what else did we find out?"

I turned back to my abandoned case notes. "Well there's Harry - we heard he was jealous of his brother?"

Toby sniffed and waved a weary paw "All younger brothers are jealous. He's a young kit not quite grown - he may make harsh words, but would hardly take a pistol to his own flesh and blood!"

I flicked on a few pages, "Then there was Thistletongue - he mentioned the entails in the will. Cecil cannot inherit until his sisters are wed. And the strange pre-nuptial agreement to protect Celia's title. "

Toby sat bolt upright, his eyes glittering, "There you have it at last Robbie - there's another motive for this wedding after all!"

"Maybe so - but I don't see how that helps us. If Cecil wants Celia wed, why on earth would he shoot her fiancee? I don't see the reason."

Toby gave me a curious look - "But it was not Julius who died, was it?"

"What?"

"You cannot have forgotten Percy my friend?"

"Certainly not - though I would give much to be able to forget that terrible sight. And the distress of his sisters. But Julius was surely the intended victim. Remember Julius was wounded as well - his shoulder was shot through."

Toby seemed downcast. He snatched up Pooters and cast it into the fire in disgust. "This is useless. Was the intention to stop the marriage? Who could want to kill Percy? Some stupid village feud?"

I poured tea for my friend. "Didn't Polly say that Percy had enemies in the village?"

"It cannot be that! What of the Petertail diamond and our recent goose-chase? Julius set us on it. What is it that he doesn't want us to see? Percy? What was he? Simply a gardener? There must be more to it."

I picked up the paper again. "Well we have another chance to investigate - Julius is back in town. The society column reports that after a recent hunting accident in Kent, the Kitduke had recovered sufficiently to return to his town residence and was expected back at his London club this weekend."

"He is certainly a weak link in this - but first we must go back to where this began."

"Oh the Great Hound's teeth! - Nottingham?"

" I fear so, Robbie. And there is but little time - we can barely make it there and back in a week. We had better set off tomorrow."

Chapter Eighteen - Highoak Manor.

I met up with Toby the next morning at the horse-stage coaching station north of London. Dawn was just breaking over the coaching house, and steam rose from the horses' flanks as they stomped about in the yard. Toby paced urgently between the carriages, picking his way between the cobbles and straw. We said little, and loaded our travelsacks into the luggage rack on the back of the coach, as the coachdogs busied themselves with the horses' tack. The coach was a large one - taking both passengers, some goods and the northern mail. We were positioned in the front section, with a view out if we wished it over the heads of the horses, and few other passengers. It was quite comfortably padded with a private dented seat, banked on each side, to cushion each passenger from the jolts of the ride. The middle section was packed - a mixture of schoolkits heading home from London adventures, earnest office clerks and solid tradescats, guarding their wares on the long journey. In the rear section, the poorest passengers sat where they could on top of boxes and barrels. On the roof, a rough canvas cover guarded the coaching staff at the front from the worst of the weather, and under a wooden and sailcloth canopy the mailsacks were chained at the back, guarded by two cats of the Royal Mail, who would sort the letters as we travelled.

We tucked ourselves into the corner of the carriage, and made ourselves as comfortable as we could beneath our quilted travel cloaks as the Head Coachdog instructed the horses to depart. The reins tautened and I braced myself for the jolt as the coach pulled away over the cobbles and onto the Great Northern Road.

Travel by stage-coach is at least rather more comfortable than by dog-coach, though it is not worth the trouble for anything other than a very long trip. I dozed pretty well on the first stretch, and was pleasantly surprised to awake at Northampton, some three

Chapter Eighteen - Highoak Manor.

hours later, as the coach stopped again to change horses. Toby and I and our sleeker travelling companions also alit from the coach to take some late breakfast at the ancient Althorp Inn. Those at the back of the coach simply yawned and stretched and chewed on dried fish.

The coachdogs are quite marvellously efficient. I observed them make the change at such a speed I had hardly time for a second helping. They whisper softly to the horses in the language that cats have never been able to master, and they slip in and out of the traces as happily as a molly slips on a diamond collar. Meanwhile one of the mailcats ran down to the local post office with a sack, while his companion soberly guarded the remaining sacks on top of the coach. He brooded darkly over his rifle. Thefts and attempted thefts upon the Royal Mail have of course been a matter of common outrage almost since its invention. Indeed, an apparent theft of just this sort had been a crucial clue in the case of the Sourclaw Emeralds. For the last two years, the Mail guards have gone armed, and after some ugly incidents where a bunch of vicious cat outlaws had been apprehended, one being fatally injured, the incidence of thefts of mail have been greatly reduced. I certainly felt more secure as a passenger knowing that our armed guards sat above us on the route.

On the second stretch, I tried to engage Hunter in conversation, but he was deep in thought and would have none of it, so I chatted instead to a grizzled old tabby gentlecat and his wife in the neighbouring settle, who were bound for a fishing holiday in Scotland. They had been some years retired, travelled a great deal and had in fact stayed near Highoak two years previously. But they knew little of interest to our case. The original family at Highoak had it seemed departed many years since, and the house was largely inaccessible, being occupied by the noble Bluefurs, with only part of its grounds open for viewing in the summer. "They are quite delightful - you should really visit them, " advised my fisherman, "enormous oaks, and rose trees quite 6 feet high!"

Chapter Eighteen - Highoak Manor.

Toby seemed still to be sleeping, shifting slightly in his seat, and hugging his forepaw over his eyes.

Finally we arrived - being high summer it was still light, and I bade farewell to our travelling companions, who were taking the night coach on further north. Toby jumped down and took the bags out from the rack, while I enquired for local lodgings. The 'Flying Horse' itself, where the horses were changed, seemed the ideal answer, and we found our way quickly up to quite comfortable small rooms.

Having rested well on the journey, Toby was eager to begin, and we made a few enquiries of the landlady and in the town before making our plans for the next day over supper.

Highoak Manor was supplied by a number of town tradesfolk, who had not been sorry to see Sir Charles and his brood depart. He had been a harsh landlord, and tight-pawed with his money. The Bluefurs who now rented the property were bigger spenders, and ran an annual fete for local villagers in the grounds. Some of the original staff of the Manor had stayed on when the Pinkpaws departed. Millicent, our hostess, had advised us that we could find many of them in the Three Mice Inn on a Tuesday evening - the staff night off. However we began by visiting Highoak Manor itself. The Manor is an astonishing ancient building, set on top of a high sandstone ridge, and surrounded by beautiful grounds. The whole building is quite square, cut from grey stone, with high sashed windows. The family house is sternly marked "Not for public access", but we paid our pennies for a guided tour of the gardens. Our guide, an elderly former gardener, was quite painfully well informed about the age and origins of almost every shrub and tree in the garden. Sadly, he was rather more interested in their histories than those of the previous occupants of the house. But he remembered them well enough.

"Sir Charles, you mean then?"

"Yes, the family that were here before. We are - distantly connected." Hunter chinked some pennies in an encouraging

Chapter Eighteen - Highoak Manor.

manner in his paw. "I was quite curious about why they left this house - it had been in the family so long. Sir Charles, I had thought, was quite sentimental about it?"

The gardener groomed his whiskers thoughtfully. "Ar, that he was. Proud, the old master was. Proud, but - if you'll pardon me sir, wicked with it."

"Wicked?"

"She was never happy here, the mistress. I loved to see her smile, too - and sometimes she would, when I brought her up roses. Her favourite flowers they were - the white ones. But he was so cruel to her. Never bothered to hide his dalliances. And he - scratched her once or twice."

"Milady Maria?"

"Ar - yes, Milady. Such a delicate thing." He wiped his eye with a muddy paw. "Twas a terrible business"

"She died in kitbirth I believe?"

"That she did. And such a pretty kitten she left behind her. I heard she's quite grown now. Ha' ye seen her? Did she grow up a beauty like her ma?"

"I don't know if she's like her - 'ma'. Certainly she is very beautiful."

"Has she her ma's brown eyes?"

"She is very beautiful. And engaged to be married this Autumn. But what happened after the tragedy? The family moved away quite quickly?"

"They could not move for a while. One of the maids had just had a litter herself and nursed the kit for Sir Charles. Then he - brought home his new bride. Indecent quick, I thought. Though he had some excuse I suppose to find a mother for the kit. But shortly after that, yes."

"Why?"

"Even a devil knows when he must hide away from his wickedness. And - he was changed after Milady died - he seemed to hate the very house."

Chapter Eighteen - Highoak Manor.

He nodded towards a rose bush "See that rose - the day after she died I found him in the garden hacking at it with a sword like a madcat- he had slashed off every flower on it - and half the bushes in the garden. When he saw me he laughed - laughed I tell you, and dropped the sword and went in. I never saw him much after that - he seemed to go quite wild. Eh - my poor mistress."

"I don't understand. Do you mean that he harmed Maria?"

"He broke her heart at any rate. 'Twas plain enough he didn't care for her. " He looked meaningfully at the pawful of pennies. "Did you want to see the strawberry patch?"

"No, I think perhaps that's enough plant life for one day. Thank you - we'll see ourselves out."

A side chamber of the great Manor house housed a tearoom, hung about with oil portraits of the Pinknose family and views of Nottingham. I supped at hot butter tea while Toby glared fiercely at the portraits, willing them to give up their clues. Three generations of Pinknoses, with their characteristic chocolate pointed fur, in a series of ancient costumes struck gloating poses, the eldest of them in a tradescat's cape and bowler hat, he was draped fatly over a barrel of seedcorn. They shared the same darkly cruel eyes and thin leering smile. There was only one portrait of Sir Charles with Milady Maria. If her portrait told true, she had indeed been stunningly beautiful, though already a fragile creature. She curled on a wicker chair next to her master, who rested a possessive paw on her flank, while gazing out over the grounds of his mansion. There were no portraits of the children, not even Celia who would have lived here, though briefly.

"Nothing of Celia, " observed Toby, echoing my thoughts. "I suppose she was still a young kitten when they moved away. Come Robbie, we had better get to the 'Three Mice' and see if there's more to this tale".

Chapter Nineteen - Three Blind Mice

The Three Mice was a raucous tavern, mostly full of servant cats from the great houses around the town, who shared the same night off. It was divided in two halves, on the left was the entrance for butlers, cooks, governesses, - the elite staff of great houses. To the right the entrance for gardeners, scullery maids, and other kitchen and household staff. There no notice to show that this was the rule, but the self-distinguishing classes of servants seemed to have decided this was so. Inside the bar, the two classes shared the same lozenge-shaped bar, that ran the length of the building, with bar staff moving around to places of greatest need - generally on the right hand side of the bar.

Toby opined that the more senior staff were most likely to have been at Highoak long enough to remember Sir Charles. We went in to to the left, and approached the bar. Behind us, small clusters of cats gathered at low old-fashioned wooden tables, chattering in low voices, clacking down dominos, or portentiously smoking oily nipbacco mixtures in curled clay pipes. From across the bar we could hear the rather louder fun of their weekday colleagues, laughing and singing and laying bets on table billiards.

Toby engaged the landlord over a cup of beer and enquired after the HighOak staff. He readily pointed them out at a prime table near the bottle-glazed window at the front of the tavern. We approached the group. Three cats sat together, one elderly tabby molly quite silently and slowly puffing on a thin grey pipe. The butler - clearly identifiable by his peppered black coat with white bib, was playing cards with a tubby marmalade-coated cat who unconsciously preened at her whiskers and licked her lips as she peered at her cards. A small pile of iron pennies sat between them, though they clearly bore a natural attraction for the bulk of their companions, which were close to the butler's elbow.

Chapter Nineteen - Three Blind Mice

"She must be the cook" whispered Toby, pointing at the ginger-coated card-player.

"Indeed," I hissed back, "losing rather badly at Cradel, by the looks of it."

A few cards were laid out in melds in front of the players. The butler still held only three cards, the tabby five, while the cook struggled to hold a dozen cards in her tubby paws. As we watched the tabby picked up the Mouse of Bones and added it with satisfaction to the two and the three in her hand, before melding them to the table. She discarded an eight of Swords leaving herself with only one card in hand - the King of Feathers.

"The death card "w hispered Toby "how appropriate!"

Toby strode boldly up to the table and clicked down a silver penny. "Good evening" he purred, pleasantly.

The card players looked up sharply, though I noticed the butlercat try to sneak a look at the tabby's cards as she set them down. "Do we know you, sir?" he snapped.

The cook laid a friendlier paw on top of the silver penny.

"Perhaps we can assist these strangers, Alfred." she purred "Are you lost, sir? In need of directions?"

"I have had the pleasure today of visiting HighOak Manor" said Toby "Such beautiful grounds."

"Ho!" said the butlercat "Not been skinned enough for one day by old Greenclaws?"

Cook hissed him quiet. "Oh Yaes," she simpered, pressing a claw hard onto the coin to test its metal, "very beautiful, ain't they. And marvellous for its fruit houses. Good productive garden it is."

"Certainly - so we were advised." smiled Toby. "And an astonishing house. It must have been converted in quite ancient times to remain so intact." He observed the greedy face of the cook as she tightened her claws on the coin. "But I was quite intrigued as to the story of the last family to live there - I understand the present occupants have only been there a few years, and there was the most delightful portrait in the tearoom. The gentlecat beside a very beautiful lady on a wicker chair. " The tabby - presumably a former ladies' maid, paused in her puffing and took the pipe from her mouth. "Milady Maria Muddlenose" she said.

Toby glanced down at the table but the coin had already disappeared. He pulled out another from his cloak-pocket and turned it in his paw whilst addressing the maid. "Was she your lady, ...madam?"

"My name is Grisel." replied the tabby. She tapped out the pipe on the side of the table and proceeded to scrape out the bowl with a thumbclaw. "What do you want to know of Milady? None have asked about her in these parts for near twenty years now." she seemed quite moved and a tear glistened in her eye.

"You knew her well?"

Grisel gave a little laugh. "Since she was barely a kitten. I brushed her coat every day, played with her mice, prepared her trousseau. I should say that I knew her, poor thing."

"Then the lady is...?"

"Dead. Dead, gone and forgotten by all that ought to have cared." she spat on the floor and muttered what sounded like a curse.

The cook laughed nervously, "Now, Grisel, 'twas sad of course, but nobody's fault that the lady died." She eyed the other twirling coin. "Milady Maria was the first wife of Sir Charles Pinknose. She died in kitbirth."

Grisel hissed at her angrily - "And what did you know of it, Gingernut? Munching your way through the kitchen stores and flirting with Alfred. What did you know?"

"Perhaps more than you think, Madam Grisel!" hissed back Gingernut, beginning to swish her tail. "I saw the Master that morning for he came down to the kitchens and gave me quite a fright. He took a fried egg right out of the pan!"

"Oh but he wasn't looking for you, there, was he?" retorted Grisel.

Chapter Nineteen - Three Blind Mice

Alfred coughed sharply. "I'm sure the gentlemen wanted no - common gossip. Perhaps I could provide a simple history of the Manor? Something the gardener would not have been familiar with?" and leaning forward he stretched towards the coin in Toby's paw.

Toby stuck it back in his pocket and laughed lightly. "Oh certainly not - gossip - dear me no. But I am quite interested in the family history, rather than that of the house. What became of the kitten?"

The servants looked at each other apprehensively. Gingernut spoke first "You mean - Celia?"

"There was only one surviving kitten, wasn't there?"

Grisel coughed and spat on the floor again. Alfred said nothing but scratched nervously on the table, scattering the cards. Gingernut affected a weak smile.

Grisel broke the silence. "You must forgive our confusion, sir. Sir Charles was very - disturbed - after Maria's death. He was - grieving - no doubt. And with the kit to consider he decided to take another wife. Which he did most - precipitately. The new mistress made a number of changes in the household. She had her own maid. She found Sir Charles - difficult. She disliked the house, and Sir Charles seemed to hate it. Neither had much time for a mewling kit. We didn't see much of her. Shortly after that - they left. So there is not much we can tell you." She pressed nipbacco into her pipe, and struck a flame in a tinderbox to light it.

Alfred clicked disapprovingly, and scraped another coin off the edge of the table into his pocket.

A practical thought struck me, "Who nursed the kit?"

Silence.

Toby raised an eyebrow and repeated my question as if they had been deaf, "Quite so - there was a wet-nurse I suppose?"

Grisel refilled her pipe and lit it - she said nothing but blinked away a tear.

Gingernut looked anxiously at Alfred for guidance and he shrugged and gathered up his cards. She jangled her iron pennies together in her paw. "My sister, sir - she had just had her own litter of two, and was able to take in another quite easily. She had been helping me in the kitchens, so Sir Charles - knew she was a helpful girl. "

Grisel coughed violently.

"Where is she now? Your sister?"I demanded

"Gillia? Also dead" Grisel muttered.

I gave my condolences to Gingernut for her loss. She smiled thinly. "Yes, it was unexpected - the flu seven winters ago."

"And her kittens?" Toby pressed

Gingernut looked embarrassed. "Well there wasn't much I could do for them - she had moved down to the south with the Pinkpaws when they went, and she had married down there, a good cat, solid sort. Had their own litter. And Lucy was such a capable kit. I thought they'd be alright. "

An ugly thought occurred to me - though looking at the plump Gingernut I could hardly credit the possibility.

"Lucy.... Marmalade?" I gaped.

Gingernut smiled broadly - "Well yes, she took her stepfather's name, so that would be her. I heard she's in a lawyer's office, though she don't write too often. Fancy you knowing her, sir - capable girl, ain't she!"

Alfred stood up. "I'm sure the - gentlecats - have heard enough of your nonsense, Ginger - hardly the Noble History, is it? Good evening to you sirs. " He bowed deeply, as only a butlercat can, and resumed his seat and his card game. Gingernut took her cue and picked up her cards. "Good evening sirs" she muttered. Grisel drew deeply on her pipe, and stared into space, saying nothing. We withdrew to the bar.

I was full of questions but Toby hushed me. "Careful, Robert, you do not know who is listening here - already we may have been too incautious. "

Chapter Nineteen - Three Blind Mice

"But ... Lucy! " I whispered. "You knew of the connection?"
"No, I did not know it - but I suspected... something of the sort. That would certainly explain her loyalty, don't you think?"
"To the Pinkpaws?"
"To their ... reputation. She must have been like a half-sister to Celia for six months or more. Though.. perhaps she might not remember it."
"Celia did not mention it."
"No - but a mother's bond - surely the wet-nurse - would not have forgotten her third child."
"Perhaps she was jealous? Celia has led a charmed life. When Charles remarried she would have returned to a life of privilege. Perhaps she regarded Celia more as a cuckoo in the nest?"
Toby looked thunderstruck. "You have something there, Robbie - you do indeed!" He snatched up his bag. "Come, Surgeon - Northampton awaits!"

Chapter Twenty - the Aldwych Dancing Rooms

One enters the Aldwych Dancing Rooms only in possession of a ticket. The tickets, of course, are to be had at a high, but not impossible price. But they are to be had only by those cats who meet with the approval of the ancient aristocratic tabbies who run the London Elegant Dancing Society - or Ledders, as society knows them.
I have never to my knowledge been much of a dancer, though I made the usual sort of efforts in that regard - at my mother's urging - in my younger days. Toby Hunter had been known to attend the Aldwych on occasion - often at the invitation of some grateful aristocratic family but if asked, I had usually demurred. The Aldwych holds powerful memories for me - I had once been engaged to a kit with whom I spent the greater part of one summer either dancing or strolling in one of London's great parks. I cannot name the Lady - for such she now is - but I may tell you that in that year I thought her the love of my life, and as yet I have no evidence that I was wrong. The Lady broke off our connection on the 15th of September, just as crimson entered the leaves. Her Mama had persuaded her that she was too young to marry. I suspect that Mama felt her daughter, who was quite the beauty, could do better than a Surgeon whose noble family no longer had an estate or inheritance to speak of. She was certainly correct, but my young heart froze a little that winter, and took some years to thaw.
I was not at all keen, therefore, to return to the Aldwych. Toby, however, now deemed it a necessary next step in the investigation. A celebratory engagement Ball was being held by the Greatclaws - all of our little cast of noble characters would be in attendance. Through the recommendation of some distant cousin, Toby had secured two tickets. We would go to the Ball.

Chapter Twenty - the Aldwych Dancing Rooms

Since our return from the north, Toby had been restless in the extreme. He had scoured legal journals for inheritance caselaw, tormented the staff of the Great Records Office for days and paced and scratched at the carpet until it was in tatters. But yesterday our tickets for the Ball had arrived, and today a great calm seemed to have descended over him. He called happily down the stairs as Mrs Neatwhisker took my cloak - "Tell our Surgeon not so grim, Mrs N, we are only going to a Dance!"

"I daresay you don't mind dancing" I grumbled "I have two left feet"

Toby looked at me curiously "Come along old chap - it has been - what - some 20 years now?"

"What has been?" I snapped. "Simply not a dancer, I tell you"

"There there - I can assure you, if it helps, that Lady Sa.."

"Do not speak Her name!"

Toby's eyes widened a little. He whistled a low tune. "Well, well - I did not think of it. I am sorry, Robbie, I am a thoughtless old tom. She won't be there, I assure you - but if it is too painful...?"

I softened - Toby and I had been friends almost since that time. He knew it all - though we never spoke of it now. "Nonsense - I'll be there. Not sure I'll scratch the Boards too deep though. Do they still have jellies?"

Toby chuckled. "I fear jellies and ice have not been the fashion in over a decade. You may have to settle for cream pudding. "

How one's heart can betray the past - I regret to say that the promise of cream pudding made all the difference.

We hailed a fast greyhound cab on the High Road, and set off for town at a little after ten o' clock. As we approached the Black Waul tunnel I lit the candles provided. If you have never taken a cab under the Black Waul it is an experience not to be missed. Moonlight and sunlight cannot be seen just 30 yards in and darkness - if you have not lit your candles - is complete. By candlelight you can see just the face of your companion, but not the racing hound in front of you, nor the sides of the tunnel.

Chapter Twenty - the Aldwych Dancing Rooms

Occasionally lights flashed past in the other direction, but for a good five minutes we were quite in the dark. Toby's face, haloed in the flickering light, turned toward me. "You must take care tonight, Rob, I have a few questions to ask, and I cannot think they would dare to violence at the Aldwych - but be on your guard."

My senses were already fizzing in the dark, alert between the sounds of the cab wheels to the scurrying of rats in the tunnel, and the rushing noise of the river overhead. The heavy scent of dog trails ran in two parallel lines throughout the tunnel, where the cabs passed in well-worn tracks. It would be no trouble to remain on guard. We turned a corner and the darkness began to lift - silvery light seeped in, rushing towards us, as we ascended out of the tunnel. The cab ran on into the town, joining an ever thicker stream of traffic heading towards the nightlife of London's heart. We passed the London Tower, and ran through onto the Thames Road. Our cabbie barked a few times at friends and relatives he passed as the traffic grew and the cab slowed to a trot. The river glowed like liquid metal in the moonlight. Clanking barges and sailing clippers jostled against the banks, and the reflected gas and candle lights of the town were jewels scattered on the water.

We pulled up by the Aldwych just as the Great Clock struck the half hour. My whiskers shook as we passed through the great glass door. Toby steadied my forepaw. "Courage, old friend. The hunt is on tonight."

Two smart butler cats collected our tickets and cloaks without a word, gave us our dancecards and nodded to the stairs. The hubbub of chattering cats drifted up from the basement. The orchestra was tuning up - plucking at violins and blowing whistlepipes. As we descended the stairway, the gong struck for the first dance and a semi-hush fell.

The years seemed to fall away before my eyes. Of course the fashions had changed a little, but still I saw before me a hundred pairs of cats, shuffling and sorting themselves into a snowflake

Chapter Twenty - the Aldwych Dancing Rooms

pattern, poised and expectant for the Dance. Young couples in love. Young kits looking for a husband. Young rogues up to no good. Cheerful couples on a cherished night away from the kittens. And ranged around the edges of the room, the older cats keeping a watchful eye on wayward sons and daughters - or on each other. And little huddles of friends, toms and mollies, laughing and gossiping together, waiting for their turn in the dance. A single chime sounded from a bell and the orchestra began. The dancers began to move, padding and scratching the boards in time, twirling and shifting the snowflake around the room and themselves turning in pairs within it. The pattern shifted as the dancers crossed and recrossed the room. Some moving fast, some slowly, but always in exquisite time with the music. I found my feet tapping in time and Toby smiling broadly at my shoulder. "Not so bad, then, eh? Have a cream pudding." and he handed me a small sugarglass pot full of set cream custard.

He was right - it is impossible to keep a bad mood in the Dance Halls. The music and the motion are transporting. I focused myself - so far as the cream pudding would allow - on the investigation. "Have you spotted the Greatclaws?"

Toby gestured casually towards the buffet table. "Getting their money's worth. I can't imagine how they afforded to hire the Aldwych if their finances are as bad as is rumoured. Credit I suppose. Appearances are everything it seems!"

I licked the inner corners of the pot. "What are we looking for exactly?"

"Who's who. The Greatclaws and the Pinknoses. Who are they with, who do they talk to? And if I can get to her alone, I want to interview Celia again. I do not think she told us the whole truth. "

He pointed to Celia across the room, glimpses appearing between the whirling dancers, as she chattered with Lillia and Noemi.

"What shall I do?"

"Those two, I think "he said, pointing out two ancient military types in the corner, sporting their campaign medals, "are of the

Chapter Twenty - the Aldwych Dancing Rooms

Greatclaw line. No doubt they have some interesting aches and pains to discuss with a medical cat. And you might get to the truth of Julius' inheritance. "

Aside from the Ledder tabbies, there were few less inviting prospects to interview in the room. But I supposed I must pay for my pudding somehow. Colonels Cuthbert and Simeon Greatclaw were two of the greatest bores - on both medical and military matters - it has ever been my misfortune to meet. The only respite was their sudden descent into silent contemplation of youth whenever an especially pretty kit whirled past. Their information on the Greatclaw fortune was no doubt accurate, if not a little dull. The family estate was partly, but not entirely mortgaged. Claw Castle itself remained family owned - though it would be unthinkable to sell it. And the rents on the estate covered the bills. In truth, there was very little money left. Enough, it seemed, for Julius to woo and wed in decent style. But after that his brothers would have to count on whatever dowry Julius could command from his bride to pay for their futures - and to reclaim some of the family estate if he could muster a high enough price. They were snobbish enough about the Pinknoses and their fortune - 'bourgeois corn merchants' - but thought the price and the accreted dignity of the fourth generation of the Pinknose line sufficient to warrant the match. Their medical ailments were too disgusting to recount.

However, one other incident of note I did observe inbetween appalling military - and domestic - anecdotes. I saw young Harry Greatclaw prowling close to the entrance, apparently waiting for someone. He looked up whenever a cream-coloured cat came in, only to turn away disappointed. Finally he got his wish - Lillia Pinkpaw came back in, side by side with her silly friend Noemi. They were chattering together and laughing, and only noticed Harry at the last moment. I could hear very little of what was said from where I sat, but Harry seemed to be pressing one of them for a dance. They seemed to be mocking him, but as he persisted

Chapter Twenty - the Aldwych Dancing Rooms

their voices were raised and he sounded almost desperate. At that point Julius joined the group, and pulled Harry away.

With revulsion churning the cream in my stomach, I sought out Toby. The third dance (a spiral) was well underway, and I could not see him at first, finally spotting him at the end of one arm of the spiral, paw to paw with Celia. The dance ended, and they bobbed tails. She chattered merrily, and he nodded and smiled. I could see Toby produce something from his waistcoat pocket, something small and shiny. He offered it to her. At first she picked it up, curious - and asked something. I could not make out a word over the chatter of the surrounding cats, dashing back and forth to book partners for the next dance. My view was obscured for a moment, and when I could see them again, Toby was speaking. Celia threw the object to the floor, her teeth bared in horror, and rushed away. Toby picked it up and stared after her, thoughtfully. He spotted me across the room, and strolled over.

"What on earth was that all about?" I demanded.

"Oh, just a little theory of mine - remember this?" and he held out his paw - nestled in the pad was a tiny gold bead.

Chapter Twenty One - Danger at the Docks

Toby would not explain the meaning of the gold bead, merely saying that Celia 'had not thought it was hers'. She seemed to disappear from the ballroom after that - at any rate we did not see her again that evening. Five dances in, the music overtook me and I offered a paw to a genteel molly who had been nodding gently and alone to the beat in a darkened corner. She accepted with a small smile, and we danced the 'two squares'. My partner must take the credit for this feat, for I could remember only half of the steps, at least in the first square. But by the second I was laughing with joy as we whirled about to the rapid drums and whistles. Beaming and breathless with success, I began to thank my partner when Toby tapped at my shoulder. "Time to go, Robbie - I think we are about to be unwelcome." He gestured to the entrance, where Julius Greatclaw was alternately glowering in our direction, and muttering rapidly to the concierge. I rapidly made my apologies and we hurried upstairs, avoiding Julius' gaze, to collect our cloaks.

As we exited the Dance Halls onto the Aldwych, there was a chill in a clear night sky. The road was full of jostling carriages, awaiting their charges within the halls. Hounds who had unhitched themselves from the traces chatted amiably and chewed on cattle bones or lapped at floormugs of hot milk. Midnight chimed on the Great Clock Tower away to the west. I scented the salty river on the breeze and marvelled for a moment at the starry sky overhead. The constellation of the Huntercat, curving his bow across the sky shone bright and clear.

"Excuse me, sir - you were left a message." one of the butlers had followed us out and waved an envelope expectantly at Toby. He disgorged a penny from his cloak pocket and took the envelope. It was blank.

Chapter Twenty One - Danger at the Docks

"You are sure this was meant for me?" He looked curiously at the butlercat.

"Oh indeed sir - the - ah - gentlecat said it was for Mister Toby Hunter - he showed me a picture of you cut from the newspaper, and I recognised you had already come in."

"An ah-gentlecat? Not quite a gentlecat then?"

"He was not attired for the Dance, sir"

"I see. Can you remember anything else of use?"

The butler mused for a moment "He was a very large cat, sir. Perhaps three inches taller than myself."

"Colouring?"

"Oh - very dark."

"Well you have been a great help, thank you!" snipped Toby. He drew a claw along the back of the envelope and slipped out the message. It was handclawed in dark ink on a rough paper.

Meet me at the Island Docks on the bridge at midnight - I know who killed Percy

Toby gasped - "At what time were you given this message, you fool?"

"About eleven o'clock, sir - but the tom didn't say it was urgent!" Toby turned to me, his face taut with strain. "Come Robbie we must fly" - he hailed a wolfhound. "Get us to the Eastern Dock yard - 5 pennies if you do it in 10 minutes!"

It was the ride of my life. Barely had we clambered in the back of the cab than the great hound pulled away with a jerk. Hounds cannot generally run at full tilt through the crowded cities, which is why the city cabs are so flimsy. I dug into the seat with all my claws as we rocketed along the Aldwych and down past the Great Temple of Bast. The London Bank flashed past on my left, as the great wolfhound bayed excitedly at his own turn of speed. I could hear greyhounds cursing him as they jumped out of our path.

Chapter Twenty One - Danger at the Docks

Toby also had a firm grip on the seat, but looked steadily ahead, over the nose of the hound and into the distance, as if he could see the docks in the distance. We turned back onto Thames Street and the stars began to race by above and below at once, reflected on the river. The cream pudding churned in my stomach, and I also fixed my gaze ahead. The traffic thinned out, and we bounced along the cobbles of Wapping and Narrow Street mainly in the dark. I tried to ask Toby who he thought the message could be from but he just flicked his tail impatiently and and muttered that he could not be sure, but that whoever we were late for could be in danger.

Finally we turned onto the Island of Dogs, and the panting hound slowed to a stop by the dock entrance.

"Twelve minutes I think - but you have earned your pennies, sir" said Toby, throwing the fivepiece into the hound's collectbox.

"Quick Robbie - take this" and as we dismounted the cab, he handed me a small pistol.

I pocketed the gun, and Toby persuaded the hound to wait a half hour - in any case he needed the rest - then we strode off into the docks.

There are three main bodies of water in the docks on the Island of Dogs. If you are not familiar with London then you may not know that the Island is really only a southern loop in the great Thames river, surrounding a spur of land on three sides. But on the northern side great square docks cut across the spur for most of its width making it almost an island. Though it is called the Island of Dogs, dogs in fact inhabit mainly the southern part below the docks area, where a forest fills much of the interior and runs up to the river edge. To the north, dockers cottages surround the exterior of the docks, while the interior is still taken up by the ruins of several ancient large towers, still not fully dismantled. One, indeed, stupendously tall, has been left deliberately as a monument and so that ships coming along the river can sight the Island docks from miles out.

Chapter Twenty One - Danger at the Docks

The docks were full of creaking ships, barges and clippers laden with exotic cargos coming in, or half loaded with goods to travel abroad. The wind whipped through the sails, and startled me at every corner. Rats rustled thickly in the shadows, scattering at our approach.

We crept along, pausing every few steps to listen for a noise. "It must be half past the hour by now" said Toby " I hope to Bast he - or she - waited". We approached the footbridge over the docks that led towards the tower. A lone figure stood on the bridge, watching us approach. A great hulking cat, cloaked and hooded, his green eyes glinted in the moonlight. As we got closer, he nodded slightly in acknowledgement. It was Shifter.

"You're late" he said.

"We came as fast as we could." I rejoined. "If you have information about Percy's death why have you said nothing until now?"

Shifter stared out at the clanking boats.

"I was born just over there" he said, pointing at a poor cottage. "Hard life, dockers have."

"What the devil has that to do with it?" I demanded, indignantly, but Toby hushed me.

"I rather think that has a lot to do with it, does it not Shifter?" said Toby

"You gentlemen know me then? Not all the gentlefolk at the house see beyond the barrels of their guns." he hissed, scratching a mark on the wooden handrail.

"I remember you were at the hunt. Is it information from that day that you have for us?"

Shifter's face turned from anger to avarice in an instant. "I may have it for you - I have it for you if you can pay?"

"How dare you!" I cried - a cat lost his life - two cats near enough, and you trifle with us over money?

"Easy for you to say, doc-tor" he snapped back " you never go short I see" and he jabbed his paw at my stomach.

Chapter Twenty One - Danger at the Docks

"Hush hush." said Toby. "Well the cat has a commodity to sell and he asks a price for it - nothing to sniff at there. But I think we must know a little more of the quality of your goods, before we open up our purses." Toby gripped my shoulder as he said this, plainly warning me to silence.

Shifter calmed a little, but still seemed nervous. "Well, my information is about - the guns"

"Ah - the guns - and what about them?" Toby pressed

"What is it worth?"

"Well - very hard to say on such a small glimpse. Perhaps...you have some more concrete proof?"

Shifter narrowed his eyes. "What sort of proof?"

"What was it you really picked up from the ground that day at the hunt? You showed me two cartridge cases, but I think in fact there was something else."

Shifter looked at him curiously. "well - there was then."

"You kept it?"

"Here - what do you make of that, detective?"

He shoved a great paw into his jacket and pulled out a tiny dark object, which he dropped into Hunter's outstretched hand.

Hunter moved under the only light on the bridge, a flickering oil lantern, to take a closer look. It was a strange acorn-shaped object, quite dark in colour.

But at that very moment a large rat chose to run between our legs across the bridge. Shifter yelled and jumped in the air - "What was that? Hell and Heaven what was that?! Have you brought police with you?"

"Certainly not dear chap, it was a rat I think!" comforted Toby - but it was too late, the tom was badly frightened.

"I knew it was not safe." he muttered, looking anxiously around. "I'm off. If you come to the house, pretend not to know me." and with that he ran off over to the north of the bridge, and disappeared into the shadows.

Chapter Twenty One - Danger at the Docks

Toby cursed rats in general, and this rat in particular, along with its parents. We had just begun to speculate as to what Shifter might know - or if it was a simple fraud, when we heard a terrible scream and splashing coming from over the bridge where he had disappeared.

We ran towards the noise, and heard more, but fainter splashing and a mewing pleading for help from the water ten feet below. I thought I heard pawsteps, dashing into the distance.

Toby took up a splinter of plank, and dipped it in a barrel of tar, left out for waterproofing. He passed it to me, gesturing to me to light it. I did so, and waved it over the water. For a while I could see nothing but blackness, and splintered reflections from the makeshift lamp. Then a movement in the water caught my eye. Shifter's face loomed briefly in the water below, shock etched in his open eyes, then disappeared, sinking into the watery blackness. Shifter was dead.

Chapter Twenty Two - Miss Marmalade again.

I had summoned a police-cat from the station north of the Island while Hunter paced angrily at the dockside. He was a typical striper - a scrawny tomcat, with roughly tabbed fur as if someone had tried to scrub out the pattern. He had the cynical eyes of a cat who had seen all the cons and vices that the East End of London had to offer. The striper was dismissive, if curious. Though I admit we gave him little enough to go on.
"He slipped, no doubt. Common enough for cats not familiar with the docks." He slid an illustrative front paw over the slime along the cobbles. "See - very dangerous, that - especially if you say he was running, sir? Why was he running, incidentally?"
I began to answer but Toby interjected; "He was startled by a rat." The striper laughed. "Well I don't know how he got here then - flew, perhaps! You can't move without tripping over a rat on this island. Friend of yours, was he?"
"An acquaintance."
"I see - well we'll hook him out in the morning - soon as the sun's up. Dockers don't like bodies floating about, spoils their breakfasts! G'Evening to you then, sirs." And with that he strolled off.
Toby quelled my indignation, pointing out that the police, who had only been in existence in London as an organised force some ten years, really had little time for probable accidents. They had mainly to intervene in murders yet to happen - brawls and such, patrolling the elegant promenades to protect the gentry, and looking to the darker, organised crimes and dens of vice of the great city.
We got back to Greenwich in record time, but the journey seemed slow - my vision was still full of that face disappearing under the water - a terrible way to go. No cat I think fears anything more than to die by drowning.

Chapter Twenty Two Miss Marmalade again.

I awoke, however, refreshed, brought to by the midday sun streaming in through the shutters of Toby's parlour, where I had napped on the couch. Mrs Neatwhisker's excellent fried kippers and steaming hot mug of tea revived my spirits almost entirely, and I scanned the morning papers waiting for Toby to complete his ablutions. He joined me, however in a cross mood - "I have not slept a wink, Surgeon - and those kippers revolt me. Two deaths now - and though this one may be even less mourned than the first I hold this blood on my paws."

"We have at least a clue." I observed, "What was that strange object that Shifter gave to us last night?"

Toby dropped the dark acorn onto the table. "I have examined it closely" he said. "I think its substance tells us something."

I sniffed it, gingerly. "It smells of.... earth! What the devil...?"

"I suspect it has been used to block the chamber of a gun. " said Toby.

"Hence Shifter's remark about the guns.... so perhaps he saw...?"

"Yes", growled Toby - "No doubt he saw someone tampering with a gun - perhaps even knew which gun. But now he can tell us neither thing."

"Julius claimed that his gun had been jammed. Perhaps someone had sabotaged it to make him an easier target?"

"Or to make sure that he couldn't fire back! But blast it, Robbie, there's another cat dead and we're no closer to catching our murderer"

"Well I don't see what more we could have done about it. Here - take a look at the paper."

Toby sat to eat, but a moment later he had jumped up again, the very hair on his tail stood up with horror. "Good Bast cat, do you not see the date?!"

"Why it's Friday - what about it?"

"Friday the 28th of August - the wedding is this Sunday!"

"Great Bast above us!"

Chapter Twenty Two - Miss Marmalade again.

Toby was pacing rapidly around the table. "I must think. Quick, Robbie get your cloak - we must be about something."

Before I could move, the bell jangled at the door and I heard Mrs Neatwhisker go to fetch our visitor.

"If it's not of moment to the case I will not see them." muttered Toby, anxiously. It was however, of very great moment to the case - for one minute later Lucy Marmalade stood before us, unbuttoning her pale blue cloak.

Toby remained tense, but smiled and offered her tea. "You are an early riser Miss Marmalade? Though even the dawn coach would surely not have got you here from Tangleburr in this time?"

"I was in London Mr Hunter - on some business for Thistletongue." said Lucy. "Thank you, no tea - I am not here on a social call."

"Pity" said Hunter. "How then may I help you?"

"You received my letter?"

"I did."

"But you did not acknowledge it?"

"I hardly knew how to reply, my dear."

"I am not your dear."

"Well then I hardly knew how to reply and it seems my luck has not improved! But tell me, d.. tell me Lucy - what has brought you here in such a huff? Surely nothing I have done?" Toby looked genuinely concerned.

"Is it... is it true that Shifter is dead?"

Toby looked thunderstruck. "How on earth do you know that?"

"I saw Mr Blackie this morning - he accompanied Milady Celia to town to assist her in shopping for her trousseau. They are staying at a hotel around the corner from my lodgings. And he told me that Shifter had - drowned."

"Did he indeed? Well, yes it is true. Did Blackie say how it had happened?"

Chapter Twenty Two - Miss Marmalade again.

"He said that Shifter had gone to the docks for - company - and that some local ruffians must have robbed him." Lucy looked rather disgusted. "Well - is it true?"

Toby waved a paw helplessly - "What should I know of it if it were, Miss Marmalade?"

"Because you seem to know everything about this dreadful business. Or you should do - you have been fishing around in it long enough! I beg you, just tell me the truth of it. Need I fear for Polly?" Lucy's cool demeanour barely changed, but the tip of her tail twitched nervously.

"Ah! I see it now. You have been afraid." Toby was soothing. "Polly is in no danger, Lucy - but the safest thing you can do is to tell me what you know."

"What I know?"

"About Celia."

Lucy didn't blink.

"Milady Celia - I don't know much that Pooters won't tell you. "

"Oh but wasn't your mother her wet-nurse?"

She gasped. "You have been to Nottingham?"

"That I have Miss Marmalade - indeed I have made acquaintance with your Aunt. She sends her regards by the way. So perhaps you might see fit to tell me the truth?"

Lucy fretted at the button of her cloak. "What did they tell you in Nottingham?"

Toby sighed - "I know that Celia was put out to nurse when Lady Maria died. She was the only kit to survive the litter and your mother had also just had a litter - presumably consisting just of yourself and Percy. So she had milk to spare for a changeling. Is that how you thought of her?"

Lucy looked up, her eyes narrowed. "She was - different from us."

"Of course - you could have seen that even as kittens. I suppose you played together at first?"

"We did."

"And at what age did Celia return to the Pinkpaw nursery?"

Chapter Twenty Two - Miss Marmalade again.

"She was five months." Lucy whispered.
"Yes - I suppose by then Lady Corcinda could take charge."
Lucy nodded, subdued.
"Did you still see her?"
"We sometimes saw her in the village. Dressed in her silks."
"Did you resent her?"
Lucy smiled. "Hardly - no. She had been - like a sister to me."
"But I think she would hardly acknowledge you as a sister now?"
"No. Is that all Mr Hunter? It was a long time ago and I cannot see that it has any bearing on the present case."
"Just one more thing - what about Percy - how did he feel about Celia?"
Tears came to Lucy's eyes. "He hated her." She stood up.
"Farewell Mr Hunter - and - be careful."

Chapter Twenty three - the Blue Lion club

Hunter was still impatient for action of some kind so we set out and headed for the park. The weather was still warm, though cooler than it had been, and a few leaves had already fallen across the paths.

Hunter strode along and scuffed crossly at the leaves. He marched us up the winding path to the lookout point where we both wordlessly stopped to take in the view. If you have never seen the view from the top of Greenwich Park then you have hardly seen London. It is quite magnificent. The lovely green sweep of the park, neatly grazer-maintained, rolls out down the hill in front of you. The stone London Towers can be seen in the west, while ahead and to the east the river loops around the Island of Dogs and off out to sea. The King's White Palace, sat proudly on the river, occupies the centre of the view. It's beautiful symmetry is matched by that of the gardens above.

My reverie was interrupted by an aggravated Hunter. "They marry this Sunday, Robbie. Two cats are dead, another frightened for her life. And I - I have done nothing to stop it."

"Hardly that, Toby - you have done a great deal. We have chased about in the dark amongst the rats and been to Nottingham and back."

"And what have I achieved, exactly? We know a little more, but nothing that explains Percy's death. I shall have to make my apologies to Polly."

We sat at the base of the statue of General Wolf whose bronze gaze perpetually surveys the view. Toby gloomily sharpened his claws on the pedestal. "Tell it back to me, Robbie - the bones of this history, and perhaps I shall see through your eyes something I have missed."

Chapter Twenty three - the Blue Lion club

We strolled up to the tea pavilion, and I obliged my friend with a history - aided by my notebook - of the salient points of our investigation.

Celia's approach to us begging us to investigate

Our trip to Talltrees, the lack of welcome from Lady Corcinda.

The Hunt - Percy's death and Julius' injury.

...Toby made me pause here, going over again the apparent locations of the various attendees at the hunt when we heard Celia's screams

our meetings with Polly and Lucy Marmalade

the details from Thistletongue of the Greatclaw debts that likely drove Julius into the need for a wealthy - though still passably noble - connection

I passed lightly over our distraction achieved by the admirable Gertie

our investigations in Nottingham - the family tree of the Pinkpaws. Shifter's approach with a claim there was something peculiar about the guns - and his untimely demise.

Toby paused and muttered to himself here and there, idly tracing patterns in the sugarbowl, but seemed to have no great leap of insight.

"And what of our protagonists?" he said "You have not described them much. What do you make of Julius?"

"Julius? Well - he is of a noble line and feels it heavy on his shoulders. He is brave - he bore his injury pretty well. Though he seemed frightened later on..."

"When?"

"When Lady Corcinda came in and found us speaking to him."

Toby laughed "Well she is a very formidable lady. I must admit to some internal quivering myself on that front! No wonder she has a firm grip on her children."

"Yes - you don't suspect them, I suppose?"

"What - Milord Cecil?"

Chapter Twenty three   the Blue Lion club

Toby shrugged "What had he to gain? Harry Greatclaw, now, he had a motive."

"What was that?"

"Jealousy - he could have been jealous of his elder brother's position in the world, and of his fiancee - perhaps he wanted her for himself."

"She is a great beauty Celia - those eyes! Like the Autumn sky. " I recalled again our first meeting with our client, and again how troubled she had been on each occasion. "I say Toby, what about that gold bead? I forgot to mention it before, but you picked it up by Percy's body - whose is that?"

"Oh I think it was Celias - I showed it to her at the Aldwych and... Great Bast!"

"What is it?"

"Robbie you have done it! Great Bast!" Toby jumped down from his chair and prowled around, muttering to himself. "Yes, it could have been done.. to avert a scandal. But then surely she would have known? Perhaps not - she need not have been told. But then which of them are in it? She cannot have been - but he?"

He leapt up and dashed the sugarbowl over. "Robbie I have been a great fool - we must see Julius at once."

"You have it? But tell me, please!"

"Not yet - I need to be sure. And there may be no way to prove it. Where could we find Julius Greatclaw at this hour?"

"At his club I should think. I believe he's at the Blue Lion."

Toby nodded "He would be. Well then let's get to the Blue Lion."

You will almost certainly not have been to the Blue Lion Club, though no doubt you will have a club of your own. Age and respectability - nobility almost, has been polished into its wood panelled walls over a century or more. The butlercats, apparently as old as the rooms, drift silently about, dispensing amber honeysuckle brandy and nipbacco refills to the dozing residents. A slightly younger crowd, who can still stay awake for an hour or so

Chapter Twenty three - the Blue Lion club

after lunch, clip each other at Cradel or billiards in side rooms, though they crow at their victories quietly, not to wake the others. Thick turkish carpets, with intricate knotted patterns in plums and yellows cover the floor, and smoke yellows the ceiling. We found Julius in the library, deep in the morning paper.

"What do you want?" he greeted us, rudely.

"Good morning, Julius - looking forward to Sunday?" returned Hunter.

He softened a little - "Not as much as Celia. I could not have believed quite so much lace could be necessary, but she assures me it is. "

"Will it be a large ceremony?"

"It seems it must be - her mother seems to think it 'the thing'. Yes, all the ghastly relatives will be there to drink in the show. "

"Not quite all, I think."

"What?"

"You heard me."

Julius sat up and threw down his paper. "Yes, I heard you - and what do you mean by it?"

"I mean that there is - at least one - sibling of Celia's that will not be in attendance."

"Cecil and Lillia will be there."

"Percy will not."

"The damn gardener?! How dare you? He was no brother to her."

"But they were brought up as brother and sister weren't they - for a time."

"Tch - nonsense - she had a wet-nurse as a tiny kit - some village molly. But she could barely remember it. She didn't know the blasted gardener any more than I did. "

"Why did he write to you then?"

Julius was dumbstruck.

"You ... how .... what do you know about that?"

Chapter Twenty three   the Blue Lion club

"Celia herself told us - when she first came to consult me. She said ... oh Robbie, your notebook please? Ah yes, 'these strange letters keep arriving that I'm not allowed to see' "

Julius considered a moment, then spat out. "He wanted money - disgusting creature. He ... insinuated that there was some obligation to his family. That now that I was to marry Celia we were somehow connected. It was nonsense - I burned them."

"You made no reply?"

"Certainly not."

"And when he saw you at the Hunt - did he approach you again?"

Julius shifted uncomfortably. "Yes. My gun was jammed and I called him over - he brought up the same nonsense again."

"He threatened you?"

"It was nonsense, I tell you. Yes - he made - some absurd threats, but I told him... where to go. He was a ruffian. Nothing to do with my beautiful girl."

"There was a struggle?"

"No. I told him I would have none of it, that's all."

"And then?"

Julius shrugged, nodding to his shoulder "Then this - I heard a crack and it all went dark. Next thing I know I've got a great hole blasted in me and Celia's shrieking fit to call up the Six-Eyed Hound himself."

"Could Percy have shot you?"

"What - deliberately you mean? No, it must have been a stray shot - an accident like Lady Corcinda said. Now I've told you what Percy wanted with me - I have dealt honestly with you. Will you leave it alone? There's nothing here for you to do."

Toby nodded slowly. "You may be right there. Very well, two more questions then. One - did you show anyone else the letters?"

"No."

"Two - Do you love Celia?"

"You offensive brute!"

Chapter Twenty three – the Blue Lion club

"Can it be such an offensive question - you are going to marry her this Sunday. Is it for money or for love? Answer me seriously Julius - it is important."

Julius fixed Toby with a steady gaze. "I love her - absolutely and without hesitation. I admit that my options were initially somewhat - constrained - by my family. But when I met my Cee ... well, none of that mattered any more. I love her."

"Then we wish you a happy marriage, sir. Good day"

Chapter Twenty Four - the Wedding

The day of the wedding dawned very bright and clear. There was no cloud in the sky, and the air, though warmed by full sun, was cut through with a hint of the Autumn chill to come.
I had questioned Toby very deeply about our meeting with Julius, "Is that it then - the shooting was an accident, Shifter slipped and fell - Celia's fears were all imaginings?"
"I have been a fool." was all he would say about it. But I could not forget that this was the day that someone had seemingly sought to - well, what? Prevent? Ensure? We had discovered a great deal, but nothing of moment at the same time. These were my reflections over my breakfast and the morning papers when I heard Toby's unmistakeable sharp rap at my door.
"Come Robbie, you must be dressed - we have a wedding to attend!"
I did not argue or bluster - I knew this determined mood too well - but took up my top hat and a fresh white collar.
Toby was already neatly attired - and very handsome he looked. Many was the sideways glance from promenading ladies as we rattled by in the open cab he had brought to my apartments.
"We are really going to the wedding, then?" I enquired, mildly.
"We are that" said Toby. "I must see it done - and then..."
"What?"
"Then it will be time for some reckoning."
He would explain no more but bade the hound go a little faster. I checked my pocket-watch - it was just gone 10 o'clock.
We dismounted the cab outside the Great Western chapel of Bast just as the bell tolled the quarter hour. The guests were mostly already inside, but an usher smiled broadly at us and sought out a flower spray as we approached. "Nearly missed it!" he began, then started as he recognised Toby.

Chapter Twenty Four - the Wedding

"Hello, Harry" he said "Oh and Cecil - good to see you doing your duty by your sister."

"I say," complained that languid cat, "I'm sure you two weren't invited. Mama has been grumbling about you half the month!"

"Quite correct, Cecil - we were not invited - but I think I am right in saying that no cat may be refused entry to a temple of Bast. "

Toby took two freesia buttonholes, and we stepped past the gaping ushers into the Temple. It is a very grand space - soaring carved columns run away down each side of the central aisle, dividing the church in three, a physical reminder of the three aspects of Bast. Set in the walls were memorials to great ancestors of great families. Cats sat in profile, fur cunningly depicted in delicate feathery strokes. Wreaths of carved and painted ivy held noble crests above them. Below our feet were the tombs themselves, set under the cold granite of the floor.

Great bunches of flowers - white lilies and pink roses - filled every recess along the aisle and their scent filled the air.

The front part of the chapel was taken up with a great mass of chattering cats, all glossed and shined for the occasion. Gemstars sparkled at the ladies' throats, and rows of top hats bobbed about between them. Toby indicated seats to the back left of the church, and we slipped in behind the least of Celia's relatives, and the senior staff of Talltrees house.

The ushers came in now, pulling-to the doors. At the front, by the altar, Julius shifted anxiously from paw to paw, casting occasional looks behind him towards the entrance where - he hoped - his bride would arrive. Lady Corcinda sat impassively in the front row, looking ahead. Her feathered hat trembled slightly in the breeze, though she did not. Julius' parents sat beside him, Duke Greatclaw in his military uniform and braided cap, the Duchess thin and impassive - with what must be the last of the family jewels around her neck.

Julius spoke to the priest, who hovered with a benevolent smile in front of the Bast statue behind the altar. He laid a reassuring paw on Julius' shoulder, gave some words of comfort, then the music started up. The bride was here.

All eyes turned to the back of the chapel - though fortunately not to us! Celia entered beside her brother - a modest lace veil covered her face, and Lillia and Noemi followed behind, wearing capes of dyed blue silk.

They walked slowly up the aisle, Celia absorbing the admiration of her peers. Her fur was brushed to a glossy shine, and as she stepped up onto the dais beside Julius, she smiled at him shyly through the lace of the veil. He gave an answering smile.

The priest coughed for a hush. He was pure black, wearing the two gold hooped earrings that are the sign of a priest of Bast.

"We are gathered today in the sight of Bast - as we are always all in the sight of Bast - to join together these two cats to a wedded state. They will promise their faithful love this day. Bast sees all. Bast will bless a happy union."

He spoke lower to the couple at the altar - "Light up your candles" Each took up a wax candle and lit it from the circular lamp on the altar.

"Behold" said the priest, "The Three Lights - the three aspects of Bast." He passed his right paw over Celia's candle, causing the flame to flicker, "The light of knowledge - wisdom and science, that casts out ignorance and darkness. "

His left paw passed over Julius' flame "The light of heat and power, that brings life to our hearths, and burns our enemies."

Then he brought his paws together and interlocked the thumbclaws over the circular lamp "And the light of love and passion, without which all other flames are useless." He took up the lamp and turned away towards the great statue of Bast. It towered over him, perhaps twice the height of an ordinary cat. Very finely carved, in sparkling black granite, it shone in the light. Images from the life of Bast, carved into the walls, ran in friezes behind the great statue. Bast himself seemed to stalk his prey around the very walls as the images, painted in shimmering

Chapter Twenty Four - the Wedding

enamel, flickered in the light. As Celia and Julius also held up their candles, the lights reflected in Bast's eyes, causing them almost to seem liquid. The priest tipped the lamp over, and a stream of flaming oil lit the tinder in the hollow around the base of the statue. At this signal, Julius and Celia threw down their candles onto the fire, and the flames leapt up around the statue.

"Now - before the flames die, you must be wed. "The priest looked solemnly out over the congregation. The ceremony had wrought its usual magic and there was a hush in the temple. "Does any cat here know of a reason why these two cats may not be wed?"

I heard a gasp from behind me - Toby and I turned to see Lucy Marmalade, in a neat tweed cloche hat. "Never fear," he whispered, "I am not here for that".

But the priest had hardly paused, "Then - Celia and Julius - link your paws - do you pledge your love?"

Celia and Julius linked their thumbclaws and turned to look at each other. Celia's veil was pushed back, and they smiled a smile of pure love at one another. "I pledge my love" they both declared.

"Then I pronounce these cats to be wed - before Bast and before this congregation of fellow cats. May their marriage be very happy."

The temple erupted with howls of congratulation and stamping of feet. Lillia and Noemi rushed up to kiss the bride. Cecil and Harry bumped noses with the groom. Lady Corcinda and the Greatclaws exchanged a gentle nodding and dipping of tails with the various noble company.

"Come, Lucy - we had better be out of here before we are noticed" said Toby, and we stepped out of the temple. "Well I know my reason," he chided her "why are you here?"

Lucy brushed a tear away from her eyes, "my family has served hers for a half century - we were never important servants.." she nodded at the cook and the governess starting to exit the temple, "but we were theirs nonetheless."

Toby quoted her back "She was like a sister to you?"

She looked directly at Toby "I wanted to be here. What about you?"

"Oh ... yes, I wanted to be here too. I had to be sure that it was right... not to stop it."

Lucy nodded "That's it - but they love each other. Why... why not?"

"Nothing there that Bast could object to." said Toby. "Go on - you have nothing to fear now." and Lucy smiled weakly at him, and stalked away.

I was open-mouthed. "What on earth was that all about?" but Toby gestured to me to be quiet. "One more thing" he said. Lady Corcinda was stood by the temple doors, hat nodding, accepting the congratulations of Milday Blueclaws. "Excuse me, Lady Corcinda," he interrupted, "but I believe I have something that is yours." Toby offered a paw - sat in it was the gold bead.

Lady Corcinda blinked slowly - she looked at the bead, then dead straight at Hunter, and nodded. She took the bead. "Thank you, Mister Hunter. As you will see I am somewhat - occupied - just now - but I see that we have something to talk about. I shall write to you. "

Toby nodded. "Thank you, my lady - I shall look forward to it."

Chapter Twenty Five - a note from a Lady

That afternoon, Hunter gave an explanation of sorts.

"You see the mistake that I made at the outset was to assume that Julius was the intended victim - in fact Percy was always intended to die."

"But why?"

"Because he was a blackmailer. Julius told us as much himself - he had written to Julius suggesting that the Greatclaw family would not much care for the connection with the Marmalades and demanding money to keep quiet."

"But as Julius said - not much of a threat surely? And Julius was injured himself - how then did he shoot Percy"

"He didn't - Lady Corcinda did"

I was stunned "Lady Corcinda?"

"Yes, she's an excellent shot. No doubt it was a little difficult to avoid Julius entirely while they struggled with the gun- but that helped her to make it look like an accident, or at worst that someone was after Julius, which of course they never were."

"But why? Even supposing Percy had exposed the connection, it was surely a trivial matter - plenty of aristocatic children have a wet-nurse. It's not as if Celia were really his sister."

"Oh but I think she was."

"What?"

"Yes - though I doubt we could ever prove it. You have remarked many times upon the lovely Celia's blue eyes, have you not?"

"Well yes, what of it?"

"But didn't you notice, in the portraits at Highoak - Lady Maria and Lord Charles both had brown eyes. Celia was not their kit."

"But then who.... - the maid?"

"Exactly - Gingernut's sister, Gillia Marmalade as she later became. Remember she had a litter of her own - well I suspect that Celia was part of that litter along with Percy and Lucy. Milady

Chapter Twenty Five — a note from a Lady

Maria died in kitbirth - perhaps it was brought on early by the shock of discovering the full extent of Lord Charles' infidelity. And in fact none of those kits had survived. But one of Gillia's kits turned out to have the looks of a Pinknose. Lord Charles took advantage of the situation. He saw a way to keep her and acknowledge her as his own - a legitimate heir. He claimed that Celia had been given to Gillia to look after, to wet-nurse. And then claimed her back into the house when enough time had passed that her true origins might not be suspected."

"So then - Lucy and Percy were full brother and sister to Celia?"

"They were - and Lucy at least must have known it. But they kept it secret for Celia's sake - even Celia I think does not know. Had the Greatclaws realised they were taking on not a bourgeois Pinkpaw, but the illegitimate child of a Pinkpaw, borne by a maidservant, the engagement would not have lasted five minutes, not least because Celia's inheritance must have been in question."

"And Lady Corcinda? She knew?"

"Yes, Lord Charles must have told her of Celia's true parentage at some point soon after their marriage. Perhaps she too noticed the discrepancy in eye colour - that is probably the reason why Milady Muddlenose's portrait can no longer be found anywhere at Talltrees and only in a forgotten outhouse in Nottingham. So she knew it and complied with Charles' wish to bring up Celia as one of their own kittens. But she must have appreciated the danger to her own brood. Celia would be difficult to marry off if ever her true status was known, and that would blight the chances of her own children.

You remember what Thistletongue told us about the Pinkpaw will? It depends of course on the exact wording, but Cecil could not inherit any money until 'all his sisters were married'. So Lady Corcinda knew it was essential to get Celia married and that her secret should never be known."

"So how did it come out?"

Chapter Twenty Five - a note from a Lady

"I don't know exactly - Percy must have guessed something, or found some old family paper after his father died, and decided to see what profit he could make from it. He wrote to Julius, who was unconvinced. He must have gone next to Lady Corcinda. She kept him quiet somehow for the while. But she decided - that he should have an accident. So she held a shooting party. "

"So who blocked Julius' gun?"

"Corcinda"

"But why?"

"Because she knew the first thing he would do - to call over the one of the huntcats - and that day she had ordered that Percy should help with the hunt. She would have Percy in plain view, handling a jammed gun. An easy shot. Easy to claim that the gun had gone off by accident. Or that a shot had gone astray."

"Great Bast! And I suppose that explains why Julius was so nervous afterwards. "

"Quite so - he gets these blackmailing letters, the blackmailer himself approaches him during a shooting party. It is all most annoying, most disturbing, and then - Bang! - all his troubles are at an end. But it must have seemed rather too convenient ... I am sure he suspected something was amiss. But he didn't want to enquire too deeply. "

"And Shifter? What happened to him?"

"He must have picked up the plug at the scene. Perhaps he had even seen Lady Corcinda do something to the guns that morning and put two and two together. Whatever he had known of Percy's game, he decided to make some easy money."

"But you surely cannot think that Lady Corcinda shoved Shifter into an East End dock?"

"No, I think Blackie did that. He does seem to be a very obliging servant, doesn't he? Tidying up after deaths, and getting rid of unruly blackmailers. Though I imagine Lady Corcinda risks yet a third drain on her finances."

Chapter Twenty Five   a note from a Lady

I was thunderstruck, and yet it all tied neatly together. A note came later that afternoon from the Lady herself.

'Dear Mr Hunter,
The object you handed me this morning was a gold bead from a brooch that I wore to the Hunt at Talltrees earlier this summer. You have been quite obstinate in investigating the matter of the unfortunate death of our gardener on that occasion, though I and others have begged you to consider it no more. I suppose that only a full explanation will persuade you to finish your investigation. My stepdaughter has now departed these shores with her bridegroom for her honeymoon and I am at liberty to speak. I beg you will call on me at Talltrees tomorrow at 11.'

"I cannot imagine how she can think to escape justice" I exclaimed, indignantly.
"Perhaps more easily than you think, Rob" said Toby. "We have no real proof of anything. I have my suspicions and theories, but the only hard evidence was a gold bead in the wrong place. It could have been lost at any time. And what good would it do to expose her? I hardly think she will murder again."
"But what about Julius? His marriage is a sham!"
"No!" exclaimed Toby angrily "You recall my last question to him? He and Celia love one another - that is all that should matter. It is all that does matter. I don't care for these noble families' nonsense about bloodlines and other such foolishness. "
I measured my words carefully - Toby himself had some murky family connection to very high nobility.
"I see - and if the next scion of the Greatclaw line has a marmalade tint to his fur?"
"Then he would not be the first!" laughed Toby "to be a - throwback, shall we say?"

Chapter Twenty Six - Talltrees again

We took the night coach to Talltrees again, and arrived too early for our appointment. We were asked to wait, and occupied ourselves strolling in the grounds. The woods where Percy had died glowered at us in the cloudy light. I found the rosebush from out of which I had first seen Percy's face and plucked the last fading red rose from the bush.
"What will you say to her?" I asked
"I don't know." said Toby "I think she can hardly be allowed to remain at liberty if I can prevent it - but I cannot see what proof I can get - unless Blackie would speak? Even then, I doubt his orders were so very specific, if he had orders at all..."
The butlercat beckoned us from the terrace - he looked as troubled as a butlercat can and still retain his official demeanour.
"Mr Hunter, Surgeon Gentlepaw, I must ... ah - Lady Corcinda will not be able to see you...ah..." the facade cracked "She's dead, sir! Dead as a toasted dormouse!"
Hunter and I gasped simultaneously. "Quick - show me!" I cried "Perhaps I can help..?"
The butlercat, whose name was Jago, began to show us up into the house, but he was already shaking his head and babbling as we walked inside "You'll not help her now, sir - She's cold - she must have - gone - last night."
Outside Lady Corcinda's room, a trembling chambermaid, cap wobbling in time with her whiskers whimpered and snuffled into a handkerchief. The butlercat knocked pointlessly on the door before letting us in.
The room was quite beautiful - thick cream carpet covered the floor, and a wide divan covered in a thick silk quilt filled the centre of the room. Broad windows showed a view out over the gardens and the woods beyond, edged by long cream velvet curtains that pooled on the floor.

Chapter Twenty Six   Talltrees again

Opposite the divan, a dressing table of white oak was topped by an oval mirror. A silver backed brush, diamond collar and various fine glass pots and potions were dotted about.

Lady Corcinda was curled up on the divan - her fine cream fur sleek and shining. She looked only asleep but a quick inspection confirmed the butlercat's diagnosis.

"How long?" asked Toby

"Since sometime last night I think - she is still stiff with the death-rigor. There is no mark on her - perhaps it was natural?"

Toby nodded cautiously, and turned to Jago "Your mistress had been ill? Why did you not check on her before now?"

"She had asked not to be disturbed. Yes, she had been ill many years - I had not known much about it but her ladies' maid knew - some internal, creeping ailment I think. Sometimes she was in great pain and could barely walk about."

"Well then," said Toby "there is nothing more we can do here - come Robbie, let us leave this house."

"What shall I do?" asked Jago

"I should speak to Macintosh - he'll know how to proceed. But do not spoil Celia's honeymoon."

We stepped out of Talltrees and walked away down the drive and into the lane. I began to speak but Toby hushed me until we were out of sight, then produced a letter from his pocket.

"This was tucked under the brush on the dressing table. I abstracted it while you were conducting your doctorly duties. I think I was justified in doing so as it was clearly intended for me."

He indicated the envelope - it was addressed 'Confidential - Mister Toby Hunter of Greenwich, London'. Toby tore open the letter and read it out.

Dear Mister Hunter

By the time you read this letter I shall be dead. I intend this evening, when I finish writing to you, to take the poppyjuice that my doctor has long prescribed to me for my aches and pains and

Chapter Twenty Six - Talltrees again

which I have been saving up for some months. I never intended, you see, that I should profit personally by my crime - everything I have done has been for my children.

I could see in your eyes when we spoke at the temple that you had found me out. I am not sure how you have done it, though I heard of your trip to Nottingham so you must by now know the reasons for it all. I ask of you nothing for myself, but for the sake of Cecil and Lillia I beg you not to destroy my reputation. I understand now that you will never rest, however, until you know the whole story, so here I shall tell it to you.

My husband, Lord Charles, was a brutal sort of cat. His first wife, I believed, had died in kitbirth. I did not know, however, until after we wed, how far his violence and abuse of that poor lady had made her life a misery. I soon got a taste of her treatment myself. Lord Charles insisted that we take in an illegitimate kit of his, mothered by a kitchen maid called Gillia Gingernut. That kit, as you must by now know, was Celia. She herself had and still has no idea of her true parentage, and has little memory of her early kithood in the care of her true mother. Soon after that, Cecil and Lillia were born, and I absorbed myself in their care. They have always been my first concern, but I felt sorry for Celia, and have always treated her as if she were also my own. As soon as the kits were old enough, Charles moved us all down from Nottingham to Talltrees - I imagine to get away from the guilt even he must have felt about Maria. The maid Gillia also came down and continued to serve in the kitchens, though Lord Charles never touched her again, out of some kind of twisted respect for the mother of his kit. But he would never acknowledge or have anything to do with the rest of that litter - indeed he insisted, though the maid and I knew differently - that Maria was Celia's mother. I protected all of the kittens from Sir Charles' rages until the day he died, and gave employ both to Percy, her own brother, and in time to Polly, a half-sister. It was perhaps strange to have them serve their own sister, but it was

Chapter Twenty Six - Talltrees again

the only charity I could shift to give the family without enraging Lord Charles, and they did not know of the true relationship. Then last year, thank Bast, Lord Charles died, after a final surfeit of drink. Before he died he had been drunk more and more often - and confessed - boasted rather - more and more of his villainy. I was relieved, but then alarmed at the contents of his will. I realised at once that if ever it was suspected that Celia was not legitimate, and not of a pure line, though I thought she could still inherit, the noble families would not readily take her in as a bride. I brought her out at once as a debutante, and she was not short of admirers. I promise you, Mr Hunter that I did not force her hand at all. The match with Julius Greatclaw was a love match - I hope that you could see that for yourself. It seemed that all might go well. And then disaster struck. Percy somehow got hold of a letter that Lord Charles had once written to his mother and got the idea of blackmail. He had always been an unpleasant kit - a temperament inherited I am sure from his father - and began to write to Julius, threatening him with exposure. Julius had no truck with Percy, but was clearly troubled, for he asked me a little about Celia's kithood. And then Percy decided to try me. He approached me one day while I was picking roses in the garden - threatened me openly that he would ruin the wedding, tell Celia, tell the world, unless I paid him. I did not think that he had real proof -there could be none, even if there had been a foolish and suggestive letter. But I could see at once that he meant to cause trouble. And that there would never be an end of it.

I knew already that I was very ill and had not long to live myself. Mr Hunter, I am not proud of it, but I decided it was better that Percy should die. I planned the Hunt party, and blocked Julius' gun beforehand, so that he could not be suspected of the attack. I stalked Percy as my prey, and waited until Julius called him over to unblock his gun. I saw a double chance as Percy stood in front of Julius - I could kill Percy and just lightly wound Julius with a

Chapter Twenty Six - Talltrees again

single shot. No one could suspect him then. I have always been a good shot. I saw my chance and took it. I do not regret it - though I admit that he was a little worse wounded than I had intended. I was grateful after all to have had you and your medical friend to hand. I practised at the same spot the week beforehand - that must have been when I lost the gold bead.

Knowing this was my plan, you will understand my horror that Celia had invited you and your friend the Surgeon to the Hunt. However I thought there was little you could do - there could be no proof it was other than an accident. Since then I have had no peace. I tried to put you off with an anonymous threatening letter. I tried to distract you with the foolish troubles of a young acquaintance. But you have been relentless, and I have had to take now the course that I knew I must always follow in the end, and exact from myself the price for my own wickedness. I beg you Mister Hunter, to respect these confidences, to accept my confession that I might otherwise have taken to the grave, and to protect my children from the sins of their parents.

Bast protect you

Lady Corcinda Pinkpaw

Chapter Twenty Seven - Lucy must decide

Toby folded up the letter and tucked it away inside his coat. For a while we walked along the lane in silence.
"What will you do?" I asked
"I don't know - I rather think, Surgeon, that if I can I shall obey the Lady's wishes. She has punished herself, has she not, beyond the likely extent of the law. We would have had no proof. As she says - why add misery to the world? Her children will have grief enough for the loss of their mother, without having to know that she was a murderess - or of the extent of their own father's villainy. But - it is not entirely my choice. I think we must ask the young lady's opinion."
"Celia? But I thought you wanted to protect her from this?"
"Not Celia - Lucy."
As Toby spoke we were already approaching Tangleburr village along the lane. It had been almost a month since we were last there, and so much had shifted since then.
We heard the buzz of the Dragon Inn down the lane to our left, then rounded the corner into the village proper. Lucy was just stepping out of Thistletongue's, she stared absently into space for a moment, lost in thought, before she saw us approaching.
She looked about to speak, but hesitated as she saw Toby's grim look.
"Miss Marmalade - I fear - we have some grave news for you. " said Toby
Lucy's eyes widened - "Polly?" she whispered
"Oh no, my dear. Not Polly - it is Lady Corcinda. She is dead."
Lucy looked ready to collapse - I steadied her arm and we steered her into the cafe where we had once eavesdropped the village gossips. We equipped ourselves with a large pot of tea, and Toby offered a few words of explanation. "We were meant to call on her Ladyship this morning. I had begun to suspect - what is set out in

Chapter Twenty Seven Lucy must decide

this letter - and she had promised us an interview. But when we arrived she was already dead - by her own hand. Here - you had better read it."

Toby handed Lady Corcinda's note over to Lucy, and she sat and puzzled over it, a slow tear welling in her eye, and coursing down the side of her nose as she read.

"But why - why have you given this to me?" she asked. "What do you intend, Mr Hunter?"

"I intend to ask your opinion Miss Marmalade. I had two commissions in this case - the first was for a murder that was in fact never intended. Celia approached me to ask my protection for Julius because she had not understood the intent behind the letters he was sent. Julius has no need of my protection unless it is to keep quiet the scandal whose true extent I believe he still has no idea of. But your half sister Polly also asked me to ensure that the murderer of your brother Percy was brought to justice. So she has been, and so I can assure Polly, but I cannot do so publicly without bringing all this to light. I believe, Lucy that you had some idea of all this long before now, and that you certainly have Polly's interests at heart. What do you think should be done?"

"Oh." Lucy looked quite overwhelmed. "Thank you, Mr Hunter. Thank you. I think... " she composed herself, took a cautious sip of tea. "I think it would be best - left in the past. "

"Very well - and Polly?"

"She will be content with your word, Mr Hunter, that Percy's murderer is no more."

"I can do that much." Hunter nodded, gravely, and took back the letter. "

" But can you tell me please Lucy - the remaining links in the story. How much did you know - and how did Percy come to blackmail Lady Corcinda?"

"I always knew that Celia and I were sisters. My mother told it to me the day that Celia left for the great house. She was so upset, and clutched me to her, crying that I would have to be her only daughter now, that I must never forget, but must never tell the secret that Celia was her true daughter also. So I always knew it, though I did not understand it as a child. Later, after Polly and William were born, when mother was very ill, I asked her about it. She knew by then what Percy was - his bad character - and bid me never to let him know in case he should do... what in fact he did! She explained to me how Lord Charles had seduced her when she first worked in his kitchens, made her great promises, and then abandoned her when she became pregnant. But she showed him Celia, the likeness no one could deny, and he wanted to take her back, to claim her. She thought - at least one child would have the privileges she would have liked for all her children. And that perhaps in time Celia could do something for the others. Later of course she knew that would never be. But at least she had been close by, had seen Celia grow up a little. And she was terribly afraid of Charles."

"And Percy?" Toby prompted, gently

"He found - a foolish letter from Sir Charles that my mother had kept. Making an assignation. It proved nothing of course, but together with the facts of her upbringing, it could have let loose rumours. He was making trouble only, there was no real proof, but he pretended there was more - claimed this was only one of a series of letters, and that there was proof Celia was illegitimate. That was what he wrote to Julius."

"And you knew that he was doing this?"

"I knew it - he boasted of it, and I could not prevent him. Julius, bless him, told him to go to - the devil. Percy was so angry..." she paused, remembering violence past. "And he determined to try Lady Corcinda."

"And that was why you guessed the true nature of his 'accident'?"

"Yes - I guessed it. And I could not blame her. Though he didn't know it, he was heading to ruin his own sister's wedding. You see - he did not realise it was really true!"

"I see. So you were quite relieved at his death."

Chapter Twenty Seven - Lucy must decide

"Terrible isn't it - but yes, I was. Lady Corcinda had always been good to our family - I thought she had guessed at - or been told the truth of it. And Lord Charles had been almost as much of a brute to her as he had been to his first wife. Percy had inherited that wicked, violent streak - after father died he ran wild. He bullied me - took half of my earnings to drink and gamble. Yes, I was relieved - I had been afraid of Percy - I feared - he would do something terrible. Then I thought there would be no more trouble. Until you began to interfere."

Hunter patted gently at her paw. " I can see now, Lucy why you wished us to leave well alone. And I can see no reason to disturb the past any further. I shall leave you a note for Polly. "

"No - I don't think you do understand - you see - Corcinda didn't know the whole truth of it. Lord Charles - killed his first wife."

"What?"

"Yes.... Milady Maria was never pregnant. When Charles knew that my mother was expecting kits, he was angry at first, and told her to - go to the devil. Near her time she left the house. Maria had become sickly, taking to her bed more and more often - worn down by his cruelty. So by the time the kits were born she had not been much seen about the estate for months. My mother told me that after she had given birth, she took Celia up to the house. Her sister who was the cook hid her in the larder, and persuaded Sir Charles to see her. He was astonished to see Celia - such a beautiful kitten - so perfect - with markings so like his own. She admitted that the rest of the litter were... well - as you see me. He promised my mother that he would help her - bade her keep Celia's existence a secret for a couple of days while he decided how to act - and took the kitten from her. But that night - Maria died. He summoned a doctor whom he bribed to say that she had given birth, and my mother's sister returned her own kitten to her to nurse."

I was gaping, but Toby spoke: "So ... who knew of this?"

Chapter Twenty Seven   Lucy must decide

"Only my mother and her sister. They were both badly frightened by what had happened. But knowing that Sir Charles was a murderer, they dared not say anything. Nothing could be proved - who would take their word? And he seemed genuinely adoring of Celia. They trusted he would help the family."

"And no one else suspected?"

"Grisel - Maria's maid - I think suspected something of it. She must have known that her mistress was not pregnant. But the doctor declared it was some strange pregnancy that had not gone well - which was why there was only one kit, and Maria had died. Who was she to argue with the doctor?"

Toby paced the room. "And you - never spoke of it either?"

"I promised my mother that it would all be kept quiet. After Charles died there was no reason to say any more. I always suspected that Corcinda had - encouraged - him to drink himself to death. Her letter tells me why - he had finally boasted to her of the whole of what he had done. But you see why I feared Percy - he had been getting more and more violent and angry. When he died I wasn't sure what to think. I thought perhaps he had been frustrated in his blackmail and intended to kill Julius - perhaps the gun had gone off in the struggle. "

"Will you still keep the secret?"

Toby reflected silently. He looked at the cat pleading him with her intelligent eyes.

"I will not - seek to make it known."

"And Lady Corcinda's letter?"

"It will be safe with me. Do you have the letter that Percy was using for blackmail?"

"No - I burned it after he died."

"Then I think our business can be done. Now eat up some herring toast, or your lunch hour will be over and no lunch eaten!"

Lucy smiled weakly, and took a bite of toast.

We left her on the steps of Thistletongue's office, letting herself back in.

Chapter Twenty Seven - Lucy must decide

"What a remarkable young lady" I said
There was an expression I rarely see on Toby's face - stronger than admiration. "Indeed so, Surgeon - a rare flower"
We ambled back up the lane together, towards the coaching inn to find our ride back to town.

......

We reviewed the case from the beginning in Toby's apartments - he paced the room and barked out corrections as I scratched into my notebook - the beginnings of this tale.

"Surgeon Gentlepaw -" said Toby, "how full is your notebook? I think I must buy you another."
"Why? Do we have another case already?"
"No - but I think we must have a proper record of this one. The facts cannot be known now - but perhaps at some future date - when all these cats are in the embrace of Bast - they should be published."

And so, reader, I have made this account of our adventure. I am sure it will not be the last.

Lightning Source UK Ltd.
Milton Keynes UK
UKOW041354130712

195931UK00001B/125/P